PERCHANCE TO DREAM

Also by Robert B. Parker
in Thorndike Large Print

Stardust
Poodle Springs (*with Raymond Chandler*)
Playmates

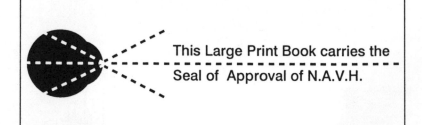

This Large Print Book carries the
Seal of Approval of N.A.V.H.

PERCHANCE TO DREAM

ROBERT B. PARKER'S SEQUEL TO RAYMOND CHANDLER'S THE BIG SLEEP

Thorndike Press • Thorndike, Maine

Library of Congress Cataloging in Publication Data:

Parker, Robert B., 1932-
Perchance to dream : Robert B. Parker's sequel to
Raymond Chandler's The big sleep.
p. cm.
ISBN 1-56054-186-5 (alk. paper : lg. print)
ISBN 1-56054-977-7 (alk. paper : lg. print : pbk.)
1. Large type books. I. Chandler, Raymond, 1888-
1959. Big sleep. II. Title.
[PS3566.A686P4   1991b]   91-3776
813'.52—dc20   CIP

Grateful acknowledgment is made to Alfred A. Knopf,
Inc. for permission to reprint excerpts from
The Big Sleep by Raymond Chandler.
Copyright 1939 by Raymond Chandler.
Copyright renewed 1967 by Helga Greene, Executrix
of the Estate of Raymond Chandler.

Thorndike Press Large Print edition published in 1991
by arrangement with G. P. Putnam's Sons.

Cover design by James B. Murray.

The tree indicium is a trademark of Thorndike Press.

This book is printed on acid-free, high opacity paper. ∞

FOR JOAN

Prologue

The gentle-eyed, horsefaced maid let me into the long gray and white upstairs sitting room with the ivory drapes tumbled extravagantly on the floor and the white carpet from wall to wall. A screen star's boudoir, a place of charm and seduction, artificial as a wooden leg. It was empty at the moment. The door closed behind me with the unnatural softness of a hospital door. A breakfast table on wheels stood by the chaise longue. Its silver glittered. There were cigarette ashes in the coffee cup. I sat down and waited. It seemed a long time before the door opened again and Vivian came in. She was in oyster-white lounging pajamas trimmed with white fur, cut as flowingly as a summer sea frothing on the beach of some small and exclusive island.

She went past me in long smooth strides and sat down on the edge of the chaise longue. There was a cigarette in her lips at the corner of her mouth. Her nails were copper red from quick to tip, without half-moons.

"So you're just a brute after all," she said quietly, staring at me. "An utter callous brute.

7

You killed a man last night. Never mind how I heard it. I heard it. And now you have to come out here and frighten my kid sister into a fit."

I didn't say a word. She began to fidget. She moved over to a slipper chair, put her head back against a white cushion that lay along the back of the chair against the wall. She blew pale gray smoke upward and watched it float toward the ceiling and come apart in wisps that were for a little while distinguishable from the air and then melted and were nothing. Then very slowly she lowered her eyes and gave me a cool hard glance.

"I don't understand you," she said. "I'm thankful as hell one of us kept his head the night before last. It's bad enough to have a bootlegger in my past. Why don't you for Christ's sake say something?"

"How is she?"

"Oh, she's all right, I suppose. Fast asleep. She always goes to sleep. What did you do to her?"

"Not a thing. I came out of the house after seeing your father and she was out in front. She had been throwing darts at a target on a tree. I went down to speak to her because I had something that belonged to her. A little revolver Owen Taylor gave her once. She took it over to Brody's place the other evening, the

8

evening he was killed. I had to take it away from her there. I didn't mention it, so perhaps you didn't know it."

The black Sternwood eyes got large and empty. It was her turn not to say anything.

"She was pleased to get her little gun back and she wanted me to teach her how to shoot and she wanted to show me the old oil wells down the hill where your family made some of its money. So we went down there and the place was pretty creepy, all rusted metal and old wood and silent wells and greasy scummy sumps. Maybe that upset her. I guess you've been there yourself. It was kind of eerie."

"Yes — it is." It was a small breathless voice now.

"So we went in there and I stuck a can up in a bull wheel for her to pop at. She threw a wingding. Looked like a mild epileptic fit to me."

"Yes." The same minute voice. "She has them once in a while. Is that all you wanted to see me about?"

"I guess you still wouldn't tell me what Eddie Mars has on you."

"Nothing at all. And I'm getting a little tired of that question," she said coldly.

"Do you know a man named Canino?"

She drew her fine black brows together in thought. "Vaguely. I seem to remember the name."

9

"Eddie Mars' triggerman. A tough hombre, they said. I guess he was. Without a little help from a lady I'd be where he is — in the morgue."

"The ladies seem to — " She stopped dead and whitened. "I can't joke about it," she said simply.

"I'm not joking, and if I seem to talk in circles, it just seems that way. It all ties together — everything. Geiger and his cute little blackmail tricks, Brody and his pictures, Eddie Mars and his roulette tables, Canino and the girl Rusty Regan didn't run away with. It all ties together. . . ."

"You tire me," she said in a dead exhausted voice. "God, how you tire me."

"I'm sorry. I'm not just fooling around trying to be clever. Your father offered me a thousand dollars this morning to find Regan. That's a lot of money to me, but I can't do it."

Her mouth jumped open. Her breath was suddenly strained and harsh.

"Give me a cigarette," she said thickly. "Why?" The pulse in her throat had begun to throb. . . .

I stood up and took the smoking cigarette from between her fingers and killed it in an ashtray. Then I took Carmen's little gun out of my pocket and laid it carefully, with exaggerated care, on her white satin knee. I bal-

10

anced it there, and stepped back with my head on one side like a window-dresser getting the effect of a new twist of a scarf around a dummy's neck.

I sat down again. She didn't move. Her eyes came down millimeter by millimeter and looked at the gun.

"It's harmless," I said. "All five chambers empty. She fired them all. She fired them all at me."

The pulse jumped wildly in her throat. Her voice tried to say something and couldn't. She swallowed.

"From a distance of five or six feet," I said. "Cute little thing isn't she? Too bad I had loaded the gun with blanks." I grinned nastily. "I had a hunch about what she would do — if she got the chance."

She brought her voice back from a long way off. "You're a horrible man," she said. "Horrible."

"Yeah. You're her big sister. What are you going to do about it?"

"You can't prove a word of it."

"Can't prove what?"

"That she fired at you. You said you were down there around the wells with her alone. You can't prove a word of what you say."

"Oh that," I said. "I wasn't thinking of trying. I was thinking of another time — when the shells in the little gun had bullets in them."

11

Her eyes were pools of darkness, much emptier than darkness.

"I was thinking of the day Regan disappeared," I said. "Late in the afternoon. When he took her down to those old wells to teach her to shoot and put up a can somewhere and told her to pop at it and stood near her while she shot. And she didn't shoot at the can. She turned the gun and shot him, just the way she tried to shoot me today, and for the same reason."

She moved a little and the gun slid off her knee and fell to the floor. It was one of the loudest sounds I have ever heard. Her eyes were riveted on my face. Her voice was a stretched whisper of agony. "Carmen! — Merciful God, Carmen! — Why?"

"Do I really have to tell you why she shot at me?"

"Yes." Her eyes were still terrible. "I'm — I'm afraid you do."

"Night before last when I got home she was in my apartment. She'd kidded the manager into letting her in to wait for me. She was in my bed — naked. I threw her out on her ear. I guess maybe Regan did the same thing to her sometime. But you can't do that to Carmen."

She drew her lips back and made a halfhearted attempt to lick them.

It made her, for a brief instant, look like a

12

frightened child. The lines of her cheeks sharpened and her hand went up slowly like an artificial hand worked by wires and its fingers closed slowly and stiffly around the white fur at her collar. They drew the fur tight against her throat. After that she just sat staring.

"Money," she croaked. "I suppose you want money."

"How much money?" I tried not to sneer.

"Fifteen thousand dollars."

I nodded. "That would be about right. That would be the established fee. That was what he had in his pockets when she shot him. That would be what Mr. Canino got for disposing of the body when you went to Eddie Mars for help. But that would be small change to what Eddie expects to collect one of these days, wouldn't it?"

She was as silent as a stone woman.

"All right," I went on heavily. "Will you take her away? Somewhere far off from here where they can handle her type, where they will keep guns and knives and fancy drinks away from her? Hell, she might even get herself cured, you know. It's been done."

She got up slowly and walked to the windows. The drapes lay in heavy ivory folds beside her feet. She stood among the folds and looked out toward the quiet darkish foothills. She stood motionless, almost blending into the drapes. Her hands hung loose at her sides. Utterly motionless hands. She turned and came back along the room and walked past me blindly. She was behind me when she caught her breath sharply and spoke.

"He's in the sump," she said. "A horrible decayed thing. I did it. I did just what you said. I went to Eddie Mars. She came home and told me about it, just like a child. She's not normal. I knew the police would get it all out of her. In a little while she would even brag about it. And if Dad knew, he would call them instantly and tell them the whole story. And sometime in that night he would die. It's not his dying — it's what he would be thinking just before he died. Rusty wasn't a bad fellow. I didn't love him. He was all right, I guess. He just didn't mean anything to me, one way or another, alive or dead, compared with keeping it from Dad."

"So you let her run around loose," I said, "getting into other jams."

"I was playing for time. Just for time. I played the wrong way, of course. I thought she might even forget it herself. I've heard they do forget what happens in those fits. Maybe she has forgotten it. I knew Eddie Mars would bleed me white, but I didn't care. I had to have help and I could only get it from somebody like him. — There have been times when I

14

hardly believed it all myself. And other times when I had to get drunk quickly — whatever time of day it was. Awfully damned quickly."

"You'll take her away," I said. "And do that awfully damned quickly."

She still had her back to me. She said softly now, "What about you?"

"Nothing about me. I'm leaving. I'll give you three days. If you're gone by then — okay. If you're not, out it comes. And don't think I don't mean that."

She turned suddenly. "I don't know what to say to you. I don't know how to begin . . ."

"Yeah. Get her out of here and see that she's watched every minute. Promise?"

"I promise . . ."

"Does Norris know?"

"He'll never tell."

"I thought he knew."

I went quickly away from her down the room and out and down the tiled staircase to the front hall. I didn't see anybody when I left. I found my hat alone this time. Outside, the bright gardens had a haunted look, as though small wild eyes were watching me from behind the bushes, as though the sunshine itself had something mysterious in its light. I got in my car and drove off down the hill.

What did it matter where you lay once you were dead? In a dirty sump or in a marble

15

tower on top of a high hill. You were dead, you were sleeping the big sleep, you were not bothered by things like that. Oil and water were the same as wind and air to you. You just slept the big sleep, not caring about the nastiness of how you died or where you fell. Me, I was part of the nastiness now. Far more a part of it than Rusty Regan was. But the old man didn't have to be. He could lie quiet in his canopied bed, with his bloodless hands folded on the sheet, waiting. His heart was a brief uncertain murmur. His thoughts were as gray as ashes. And in a little while he too, like Rusty Regan, would be sleeping the big sleep. . . .

1

The water looped out of the hose in a long lazy silver sluice as the Japanese gardener played it over the emerald lawn. The Sternwood house looked the same.

The general had died. Which was too bad. And Eddie Mars hadn't died, which was also too bad. And Carmen had been put away. But Vivian was still there. And Norris the butler was still there. He had called me and asked me to come out.

The place was full of remembrance. The same low solid foothills rose behind the house. The same terraced lawn dropped the long easy drop down to the barely visible oil derricks where a few barrels a day still creaked out of the ground. The sun shone on the olive trees and vivified the birds that fluttered among the leaves. The birds sang as if the world were still young.

Which it wasn't.

Norris answered my ring. He was tall and silver-haired, a vigorous sixty with the pink skin of a man whose circulation was good.

"Mr. Marlowe," he said. "Good of you to come."

The hallway was the same as it had been the first time I saw it. The portrait of the hot-eyed ancestor over the mantel. The knight and the lady forever still in the stained-glass window. The knight always trying to untie her. The lady always captive. The lady was still naked. The hair still conveniently long. It had been a while since I had first stood here and Carmen Sternwood had told me I was tall and pitched into my arms. Only yesterday.

She was twenty or so, small and delicately put together, but she looked durable. She wore pale blue slacks and they looked well on her. She walked as if she were floating. Her hair was a fine tawny wave cut much shorter than the current fashion of pageboy tresses curled in at the bottom. Her eyes were slate gray, and had almost no expression when they looked at me. She came over near me and smiled with her mouth and she had little sharp predatory teeth, as white as fresh orange pith and as shiny as porcelain. They glistened between her thin too taut lips. Her face lacked color and didn't look too healthy.

"Tall, aren't you?" she said.

"I didn't mean to be."

Her eyes rounded. She was puzzled. She was thinking. I could see, even on that short acquaintance, that thinking was always going to be a bother to her.

"Handsome too," she said. "And I bet you know it."

I grunted.

"What's your name?"

"Reilly," I said. "Doghouse Reilly."

"That's a funny name." She bit her lip and turned her head a little and looked at me along her eyes. Then she lowered her lashes until they almost cuddled her cheeks and slowly raised them again, like a theater curtain. I was to get to know that trick. That was supposed to make me roll over on my back with all four paws in the air.

"Are you a prizefighter?" she asked, when I didn't.

"Not exactly. I'm a sleuth."

"A — a — " She tossed her head angrily, and the rich color of it glistened in the rather dim light of the big hall. "You're making fun of me."

"Uh-uh."

"What?"

"Get on with you," I said. "You heard me."

"You didn't say anything. You're just a big tease." She put a thumb up and bit it.

It was a curiously shaped thumb, thin and narrow like an extra finger, with no curve in the first joint. She bit it and sucked it slowly, turning it around in her mouth like a baby with a comforter.

"You're awfully tall," she said. Then she giggled with secret merriment. Then she turned her body slowly and lithely, without lifting her feet. Her hands dropped limp at her sides. She tilted herself toward me on her toes. She fell straight back into my arms. I had to catch her or let her crack her head on the tessellated floor. I caught her under her arms and she went rubber-legged on me instantly. I had to hold her close to hold her up. When her head was against my chest she screwed it around and giggled at me.

"You're cute," she giggled. "I'm cute too."

I didn't say anything. So the butler chose that convenient moment to come back through the French doors and see me holding her.

Well, maybe not quite yesterday.

I followed Norris's straight back down the same corridor toward the French doors. The house seemed quieter now. Probably my imagination. It was too big a house and too chilled with sadness ever to have been noisy. This time, we turned under the stairs and

20

went down some stairs to the kitchen. The horsefaced maid was there. She smiled and bobbed her head at me. Norris glanced at her and she bobbed her head again and went out of the kitchen.

The kitchen was big and opened out onto the back lawn as it dropped away from the house. Like so many hillside mansions in Los Angeles the first floor in front was the second floor in back. The floors were a polished brown Mexican tile. There was a large wooden worktable in the center of the room, a big professional-looking cookstove against the far wall, two refrigerators to the right, and a long counter with two sinks and a set tub along the left wall.

"Will you have coffee, sir?" Norris said.

I said I would and Norris disappeared into a pantry off the kitchen and returned in a moment with a silver coffee service and a bone china cup and saucer. He poured the coffee into the cup in front of me. And placed an ashtray nearby.

"Please smoke if you wish to, Mr. Marlowe," Norris said.

I sipped the coffee, got out a cigarette and lit it with a kitchen match.

"How are the girls?" I said.

Norris smiled.

"The very subject I wished to discuss, sir."

21

Norris stood erect beside the table. I waited.

"The General used to like brandy in his coffee, sir," Norris said. "Would you care for some?"

"Join me," I said.

Norris started to shake his head.

"For the General," I said. Norris nodded, got another cup, put brandy in my cup and a splash, straight, in his cup.

He raised his cup toward me.

"To General Guy Sternwood," he said, giving "Guy" the French pronunciation.

I raised my cup back.

"General Sternwood," I said. I had first met him in the greenhouse, at the foot of the velvet lawn.

The air was thick, wet, steamy and larded with the cloying smell of tropical orchids in bloom . . . after a while we came to a clearing in the middle of the jungle, under the domed roof. Here, in a space of hexagonal flags, an old red Turkish rug was laid down and on the rug was a wheelchair and in the wheelchair an old and obviously dying man watched us come with black eyes from which all fire had died long ago, but which still had the coal-black directness of the eyes in the portrait that hung over the mantel

22

in the hall. The rest of his face was a leaden mask, with the bloodless lips and the sharp nose and the sunken temples and the outward-turning earlobes of approaching dissolution. His long narrow body was wrapped — in that heat — in a traveling rug and a faded red bathrobe. His thin claw-like hands were folded loosely on the rug, purple nailed. A few locks of dry white hair clung to his scalp, like wild flowers fighting for life on a bare rock.

I sipped my coffee. Norris took a discreet drink of his brandy. There was no sound in the big kitchen. The General's ghost was with us, and both of us were quiet in its presence.

"What do you know about my family?"
"I'm told you are a widower and have two young daughters, both pretty and both wild. One of them has been married three times, the last time to an ex-bootlegger who went in the trade by the name of Rusty Regan. That's all I heard, General. . . ."

"I'm afraid Miss Carmen has disappeared," Norris said, interrupting my thoughts.
"From where?" I said.
"After that, ah, misfortune with Rusty

23

Regan," Norris said, "Miss Vivian placed her in a sanitarium as, I believe, you advised her to."

I nodded. The coffee was strong and too hot to drink except in small sips. The brandy lay atop the coffee and made a different kind of warmth when I sipped it. I could hear the General's voice thin with age, taut with feeling long denied.

"Vivian is spoiled, exacting, smart, and quite ruthless. Carmen is a child who likes to pull wings off flies. Neither of them has any more moral sense than a cat. Neither have I. . . ."

There was another sound in the voice. Besides the tiredness and the iron self-control, there was a wistful sound, a sound of what might have been, a sound of sins revisited but irredeemable. And it was that sound which held me, as I knew it held Norris, if only in memory, long after the speaker had fallen silent.

"Vivian went to good schools of the snob type and to college. Carmen went to half a dozen schools of greater and greater liberality, and ended up where she started. I presume they both had, and still have, all

the usual vices. If I sound a little sinister as a parent, Mr. Marlowe, it is because my hold on life is too slight to include any Victorian hypocrisy." He leaned his head back and closed his eyes, then opened them again suddenly. "I need not add that a man who indulges in parenthood for the first time at the age of fifty-four deserves all he gets. . . ."

"She was doing very well at the sanitarium," Norris said. "I myself had the privilege of visiting her every week."

"And Vivian?" I said. The daughters' names seemed to dispel the father's ghost.

"Miss Vivian visited whenever she was, ah, able." Norris turned the cup slowly in his clean strong hands. "Her father's death was difficult for her. And she is still seeing Mr. Mars."

Norris's voice was careful when he said it, empty of any evaluation. The voice of the perfect servant, not thinking, merely recording.

"How nice for her," I said. "Did she tell you to call me?"

"No, sir. I took that liberty. Miss Vivian feels that Mr. Mars will find Miss Carmen and return her to the sanitarium."

"His price will be higher than mine," I said.

"Exactly so, sir."

"And you know what I charge?"

"Yes, sir. You'll recall that I handled the General's checkbook for him when he employed you previously."

"And you can afford me?"

"The General was very generous to me in his will, sir."

I took a lungful of smoke and let it out slowly and tilted my chair on its back legs.

"But still you're working here," I said.

"I believe the General would have wished that, sir. His daughters . . ." Norris let the rest of the sentence disappear into an eloquent servant's self-effacement.

"Yes," I said. "I'm sure he would have. When did Carmen disappear?"

"A week ago. I went on my weekly visit and found that she was gone. The staff was somewhat reticent about her disappearance, but I was able to ascertain that she had in fact been gone for at least two nights."

"And no one had reported it?"

"Apparently not, sir. I informed Miss Vivian Sternwood, of course, and took the liberty of speaking on the telephone with Captain Gregory of the Missing Persons Bureau."

"And?" I said.

"And it was, as I remember his words, 'the first I'd heard of it.' "

26

"And Vivian?" I said.

"Miss Vivian said that I was not to worry about it. That she had resources and that Carmen would turn up."

"And by 'resources,' you understood her to mean Eddie Mars?" I said.

"I did, sir."

"How does she feel about you calling me?" I said.

"I have not yet informed her of that, sir."

I drank the rest of the coffee laced with brandy. It had cooled enough to go down softly. I nodded more to myself than to Norris.

"What is the name of this sanitarium?" I said.

"Resthaven, sir. It is supervised by a Dr. Bonsentir."

"Okay," I said, "I'll take a run out there."

"Yes, sir," Norris said. "Thank you very much, sir. May I give you a retainer?"

"A dollar will do for now," I said. "Make it official. We'll talk about the rest of it later."

"That's very kind indeed, sir," Norris said. He took a long pale leather wallet out of his inside pocket and extracted a dollar bill and gave it to me. I wrote him out a receipt, took the bill, and put it in my pocket, negligently, like there were many more in there and I had no need to think about it.

"May I call you here?" I said.

"Indeed, sir. I often receive calls here. Answering the phone is normally among my duties."

"And how is Vivian?" I said.

"She is still very beautiful, sir, if I may be so bold."

"And still dating a loonigan," I said.

"If you mean Mr. Mars, sir, I'm afraid that is the case."

2

I came out of the Sternwood house and stood on the front stoop with my hat in my hand, holding it by the brim against my right thigh. Below me, many terraced levels down the hill, was the big spiked fence that separated the Sternwoods, or what was left of them, from the people who still worked for a living. The sun glinted off the gilt spear points of the fence. To the north it shone on the snow in the San Gabriel Mountains. I looked back down the lawn the other way, at the few creaking oil derricks still tiredly pumping five or six barrels a day. It was hard to see them from here, and impossible to see beyond them to the stinking sump where Rusty Regan lay dreamless, sleeping the big sleep.

Behind me the door opened.

"Marlowe?"

I turned and looked at Vivian Regan, the General's older daughter, the one with the hot eyes and the sulky mouth and the great legs. She was in some kind of white silk lounging outfit today; a bell-sleeved silk top with a plunging neckline and wide floppy silk pants that hid the great legs but hinted to you that if you got a look they would indeed be great. She had an unlighted cigarette in her mouth.

"Got a match?" she said and leaned a little toward me through the open door.

I dug out a kitchen match and snapped it on my thumbnail and lit her cigarette.

"Still a masterful brute, aren't you," she said.

I didn't want to say I wasn't, so I let it drift with the aimless current of Sternwood life.

"Still sitting in the window," I said, "peeking through the curtains?"

"I live here, Marlowe, or had you forgotten? I like to know who's going in and out."

"I came in a while ago," I said. "Now I'm going out."

Vivian stepped through the door and closed it behind her. She took in some smoke and held it a long time and then let it trail out slowly as she stared down at the distant line of derricks.

"A walk down memory lane, Mr. Marlowe? Or perhaps you came courting and lost your nerve?"

I shook my head.

"Still the strong silent type, aren't you?"

I grinned at her and nodded and put my

30

hat on with the brim tipped forward over my forehead. I moved off the front step and began to move along down the slope toward my car. Vivian came along with me. I could feel the tension in her. Her movements were jagged with it.

"You talked with Eddie Mars," she said.

"Sure, after the Regan thing. I said I would."

"How'd he take it?"

"You know I talked with him," I said. "You probably know how he took it."

"You told him to stay away from me, and from Carmen. You said my father was never to know and if he found out, you, personally, would find a way to put Eddie upstate for a long time."

"Just making small talk," I said. "I hope I didn't upset him."

"Eddie Mars? It would take more than a cut-rate gumshoe to scare Eddie Mars."

"I charge full rates," I said. "And your father died without knowing."

"Yes," she said. "He did."

The tight planes of her face softened for a moment. She put her hand on my arm as we walked along the brick pathway toward the gate.

"I'm grateful for that, Marlowe."

I said "Uh huh."

We were almost at the gate. I had parked my car under a pepper tree on the street, the same way I had the first time, that October when I'd come to call with the look of hard rain in the foothills, because Bernie Ohls, the DA's chief investigator, had told me that General Sternwood needed a gumshoe.

"Why are you here, Marlowe?"

"I came to call on your butler," I said.

"Without consulting me?"

"This is southern California, Mrs. Regan, in the twentieth century. Servants are now employees, not slaves. I know you don't like that, but you'll have to face it sooner or later."

She tried to slap me, but I got a forearm up between my face and her hand.

"Bastard," she said.

"How's Carmen?" I said.

"Fine," Vivian said.

"I doubt that," I said. "She wasn't fine the last time I saw her, when she tried to put five bullets in me like she did Regan."

"I did what you said, you know that. I took her away. We went to Switzerland, she took some treatments."

"And now you're back," I said. "And where's Carmen?"

"In a sanitarium," Vivian said.

"Resthaven?"

Vivian gave me a sharp look. The skin seemed to be stretched too tight over her cheekbones.

"What has Norris told you?" she said.

"Privileged communication," I said. "What are you doing to find her?"

"That bastard," Vivian said. "He told you, didn't he?"

"She shouldn't be running around loose," I said.

"She's all right. I've got people looking for her."

"Mars?" I said.

"Eddie has promised to find her. She's probably just run off with some man. You know how Carmen is."

Vivian was as casually unconcerned as a butterfly on a tulip.

"She met this guy she must have run off with at a party at the sanitarium?"

"Don't be sarcastic, darling. It's so trite. They have sheltered social activity at the sanitarium. Dr. Bonsentir is very progressive."

"I'll bet he is," I said. "How did you find him?"

"He came highly recommended," Vivian said.

"By who?" I said. "Eddie Mars?"

"Damn you, Marlowe, why are you so down on Eddie? Since Father died he has

33

been a good friend."

"Mars is a gambler, a thug, a murderer by proxy, a thief, probably a pimp. If he's a good friend to anyone it's Eddie Mars, anyone else is just raw material," I said.

Vivian dropped the cigarette I'd lit for her and ground it into the brick walk with the toe of a pink slipper. She looked up at me and her eyes had the hot look I remembered. The look was probably part of the Sternwood blood and made for heroism at its best and debauchery on a gaudy scale at its worst.

"I'm sick of you, Marlowe. I'm sick of your face. I'm sick of you in my life. I'm sick of you preaching at me, and moralizing, and acting like you were something better than I am, when all you are is a second-rate shoofly with a lousy office in a crummy section of town and two suits of clothes. I could buy fifty of you and use you around the house for bookends."

She turned and stamped back up the brick walk, looking for a door to slam. She didn't find one until she reached the house, and when she did she went inside and slammed it.

A hummingbird hovered in frantic suspension over a flowering azalea near the gate.

"Probably doesn't have enough books," I

said to the hummingbird.

He paid no attention to me. I shrugged and went out and got in my car and headed back toward my lousy office, in the crummy part of town.

3

The first time I had met Vivian Regan I had come to see her father, who wanted me to take a blackmailer off his back. She was still married to Rusty Regan who, it was said, used to command a brigade in the Irish Republican Army. But Rusty had disappeared, and the General missed him. I thought at the time, and still think, that the General hired me to make sure the blackmailer wasn't Rusty Regan. If it had been, which it wasn't, it would have broken his heart. When I left the General that day with my shirt sticking to my back and the sweat soaking my collar, Norris told me that Mrs. Regan wanted to see me.

I sat down on the edge of a deep soft chair and looked at Mrs. Regan. She was worth a stare. She was trouble. She was stretched out on a modernistic chaise longue with her slippers off, so I stared at her legs in the sheerest silk stockings. They seemed to be arranged to stare at. They were visible to the knee and one of them well beyond.

The knees were dimpled, not bony and sharp. The calves were beautiful, the ankles long and slim with enough melodic line for a tone poem. She was tall and rangy and strong looking. Her head was against an ivory satin cushion. Her hair was black and wiry and parted in the middle and she had the hot black eyes of the portrait in the hall. She had a good mouth and a good chin. There was a sulky droop to her lips and the lower lip was full. . . .

She had wanted to know if her father had hired me to find Rusty Regan. Since she hadn't hired me it was none of her business. I wouldn't tell her. She didn't like that.

She flushed. Her hot black eyes looked mad. "I don't see what there is to be cagey about," she snapped. "And I don't like your manners."

"I'm not crazy about yours," I said. "I didn't ask to see you. You sent for me. I don't mind you ritzing me or drinking your lunch out of a scotch bottle. I don't mind you showing me your legs. They're very swell legs and it's a pleasure to make their acquaintance. I don't mind if you don't like my manners. They're pretty bad. I grieve over them during the long winter evenings.

But don't waste your time trying to cross-examine me."

She slammed her glass down so hard it slopped over on an ivory cushion. She swung her legs to the floor and stood up with her eyes sparking fire and her nostrils wide. Her mouth was open and her bright teeth glared at me. Her knuckles were white. "People don't talk like that to me," she said thickly.

I sat and grinned at her. Very slowly she closed her mouth and looked down at the spilled liquor. She sat down on the edge of the chaise longue and cupped her chin in one hand.

"My God, you big dark handsome brute! I ought to throw a Buick at you. . . ."

The rain had come hard that day, and it would come again another day. But today, thinking about Vivian, I drove in hot sunlight back toward Hollywood.

There had always been that between us, the harsh edge of wilfulness, grating against the insistent push of desire. It had obsessed us then, and I could feel it now, the push and pull of it between us.

The blackmailing wasn't much, some uncollectable IOUs to a man named Geiger. I could have cleaned that up in an afternoon if I could have gotten to Geiger. But I couldn't until it was too late, and then it was really too late.

On a sort of low dais at one end of the room was a high-backed teakwood chair in which Miss Carmen Sternwood was sitting on a fringed orange shawl. She was sitting very straight, with her hands on the arms of the chair, her knees close together, her body stiffly erect in the pose of an Egyptian goddess, her chin level, her small white teeth shining between her parted lips. Her eyes were wide open. The dark slate color of the iris had devoured the pupil. They were mad eyes. She seemed to be unconscious. She looked as if, in her mind, she was doing something very important and making a fine job of it. Out of her mouth came a tinny chuckling noise, which didn't fit her expression or even move her lips.

She was wearing a pair of long jade earrings. They were nice earrings and had probably cost a couple of hundred dollars. She wasn't wearing anything else. . . .

I stopped looking at her and looked at Geiger. He was on his back on the floor, beyond the fringe of the Chinese rug, in front of a thing that looked like a totem pole. It had a profile like an eagle and in *its wide round eye was a camera lens. The lens was aimed at the naked girl in the chair. There was a blackened flash bulb clipped to the side of the totem pole. Geiger was wearing Chinese slippers with thick felt soles, and his legs were in black satin pajamas and the upper part of him wore a Chinese embroidered coat, the front of which was mostly blood. His glass eye shone brightly up at me and was by far the most lifelike thing about him. At a glance none of the three shots I heard had missed. He was very dead. . . .*

A lot of people had died since then. And here we were, the survivors, circling still in some sort of aimless ritual around little Carmen. The thought made me need a drink and when I got to my office I sat alone at my desk and had one. It didn't do any good. On the other hand it did no great harm either.

4

Resthaven sprawled in a small canyon that ran laterally off of Coldwater Canyon, just below Mulholland Drive. Some movie magnate had built it once in the late twenties, probably with the first big wad of pre-income tax money that he'd made filming two-reelers in Topanga Canyon. It might have been a ranch if you could picture a ranch built to specification for a Middle European peddler who'd struck it rich. It had a main building made of peeled redwood logs, squared and notched and fitted as snug as wallpaper. There was the bunkhouse, a longer lower echo of the main house, and there were three or four outbuildings which followed the same motif.

Like most of southern California, the land, if left to its own devices, would have been dry and ugly. But it hadn't been left to its own devices. It had been watered and planted and pruned and fertilized and a profusion of flowering shrubs splashed across the green lawn and flanked the crushed shell driveway that curved up to the main entrance. There was no one in sight. And only a discreet sign burned into a polished square of redwood said RESTHAVEN. I parked under a big old eucalyptus tree that the wind had tortured into a posture of contorted abandon, and crunched across the driveway to ring the bell.

The bell was soft, a lilting little chime deep somewhere in the house. Out of sight, maybe around the corner, I could hear dimly the sound of a sprinkler clicking in slow cadence as it arched back and forth. There was a trumpet vine curling up around the support pillars on the rustic porch. I waited, listening for footsteps and heard none, and then the door opened and a pale man with thin shoulders and very slick black hair combed straight back stood there.

"Marlowe," I said. "To see Dr. Bonsentir."

I handed him my card. The quiet one, name, address, profession. The one with the crossed sabers I saved for impressing other clients. The guy in the white coat ushered me into a hallway that was dark and cool. There were Navaho rugs strewn on the polished wide board floors. Framed on the walls were a variety of important-looking medical documents, some plaques honoring various civic achievements and a head shot of Dr. Bonsentir himself with a lot of uplighting, and some artful air brushing. A small brass plaque under the photograph said OUR FOUNDER, DR. CLAUDE BONSENTIR.

The servant left me there to admire Dr. Claude and returned in maybe two minutes.

"This way, sir," he said with the faint hint of an accent, though I couldn't identify it.

I followed him through a door to the right. We went through a room that was probably a library, with books in shelves along all of the paneled walls and a vast stone fireplace against the far end of the room. There were drapes on all the windows in some sort of turquoise coloration that reached the floor and gathered in an overabundant pile at the baseboard. Beyond the library was an office, smaller than the library but done in the same motif and complete with a slightly scaled-down version of the same fieldstone fireplace on the near end wall where it could share the same chimney shaft. In here the turquoise drapes were drawn and the room was dim. In front of the windows was a desk that could have been a basketball court for midgets. And behind it was Claude Bonsentir.

He was a dark lean jasper with longish black hair parted in the exact middle of his head. He wore a pencil moustache, and his dark eyes were deeply recessed so that he seemed to be peering out at you from far inside someplace. He was wearing a dark suit with a wide white pinstripe. There was a big gold watch chain draped across his vest, and some sort of key hung from it. He sat with his hands tented before him, elbows on the desk. His nails were manicured and gleamed with recent buffing. He tapped his fingertips gently against his lower lip. On the desk before him, set at precise square to him, was my card. There was nothing else on the desk top except an onyx pen and pencil set. He stared down at my card. I stood in front of his desk. He continued to stare down at my card. I waited.

Across the room there were two leather chairs with brass studding along the seams, and squarish arms. I went over and got one and dragged it to his desk and sat in it across from him. He raised his eyes slowly and peered out at me from the deep sockets.

I waited. He gazed.

I said, "You want to check my teeth?"

Bonsentir did not smile, nor did his gaze waver.

"You are a private detective," he said. He had one of those Hollywood elocution voices which has no real accent but sounds nearly British, especially if you haven't heard a real one. He sounded like a guy that recited

44

bad poems on the radio.

"When I'm not polishing my yacht," I said.

Bonsentir did some more gazing. I waited. As my eyes got accustomed to the dimness I could see that the walls were ornamented with some sort of Indian metalwork. Turquoise and stones I couldn't recognize set in patterns on a large silver shield. There were six or seven of these around the office. Over the fireplace was a big oil painting of Bonsentir, wearing a white robe and looking profound.

"I am a serious man, Mr. Marlowe. I have the well-being of many people in my purview. I devote my time to thinking about them. I have no time left over to be amusing."

"You're doing okay," I said.

He raised an eyebrow. "You find me amusing," he said.

"Enthralling," I said. "I was wondering if you could tell me the whereabouts of Carmen Sternwood?"

Bonsentir leaned back slowly in his chair and opened his mouth wide enough so he could tap his lower teeth with his thumbs. He worked the gaze on me some more. I think it was supposed to make me melt into a puddle on the floor near his desk.

"Why do you ask?" Bonsentir said.

"I've been employed to ask," I said.

"By whom?"

"By he who employed me," I said.

"He?"

"He or she," I said.

"May I have this person's name?" Bonsentir said.

"Why?" I said.

Bonsentir dropped his hands to the desk top and let them lie flat. He leaned forward slightly.

"You are very annoying, Mr. Marlowe."

"I've heard that," I said. "I have often resolved to improve."

Bonsentir kept his new pose.

"I'm afraid the well-being of my patient requires me to turn aside all unauthorized inquiries, Mr. Marlowe. I greatly respect each patient's right to privacy."

"She's here then?" I said.

"I cannot comment on any of your questions, I'm afraid."

"I heard she wasn't here," I said. "I heard that she's gone and that her sister, Vivian Regan, has asked a hard customer named Eddie Mars to find her."

"Do you represent Mrs. Regan?"

"No. I represent her butler."

"Her butler?" Bonsentir came as close as he probably could to laughing. It made his

46

pencil moustache wiggle slightly.

"My dear Mr. Marlowe, I'm very dreadfully afraid that Mrs. Regan's butler has very little standing here."

"Doctor, there's a couple of ways we can go with this," I said. "You could cooperate by either showing me Carmen Sternwood alive and well, or explaining to me where she is, and helping me find her; or I can come up here with a couple of tough L.A. County deputies and stomp all over your jonquils and interrogate your staff and probably set your patients back five years. Cops are kind of direct sometimes."

"I assure you, Marlowe, that would be a mistake," Bonsentir said. "I am not without knowledge of my legal rights, and I am not without influence."

"But you seem to be without Carmen Sternwood," I said.

"It is time for you to leave, Marlowe."

Bonsentir pressed a button under the rim of his desk and the door to his office opened and two guys in white came in. One of them was a blond beachboy. His hair almost white, his skin where he bulged out of his white T-shirt, a golden tan. I could have taken him with a swizzle stick.

The other guy was trouble. He was Mexican, with opaque black eyes that were all

47

Indian and thick black hair that he had pulled back and tied in a pigtail. His arms were unnaturally long and his legs seemed short, and bowed; too small to support the massive upper half of him.

"My orderlies will show you out now."

I could see that they would. I stood up.

"I'm going to find Carmen Sternwood," I said to Bonsentir. "You better hope I find her here."

"Mr. Marlowe, you are a little man doing a little man's pallid job. Don't waste your time trying to threaten me. It is time now for you to go."

The two orderlies stood beside me, looking at Bonsentir. I could smell whatever the Mexican had eaten for lunch. I looked at Bonsentir and shrugged and headed for the door. The orderlies followed me out and to my car and stood in the driveway watching me until I was out of sight. When I reached Sunset I headed east toward downtown L.A. Scaring Dr. Bonsentir out of his wits hadn't been too effective. Time to try a different approach.

5

Captain Gregory of the Missing Persons Bureau shifted his heavy body in his swivel chair and looked at me as carefully as he did everything else.

"How you been, Marlowe?" he said.

He had a thick bulldog pipe in his hands and was packing tobacco into the bowl from a canister on his desk.

"Nobody's hit me with a sap this month," I said.

"Surprising," Gregory said.

"Month's not over yet," I said.

Gregory had the pipe packed the way he wanted it. He put it in his mouth and lit it with a kitchen match, moving the match carefully over the surface of the tobacco to make sure it was evenly lit. He drew in a big draught of smoke and blew the match out with it. Behind him through his office window I could see the hall of justice maybe half a mile away.

"Never found Rusty Regan, I guess," Gregory said.

"Never laid eyes on him," I said.

Gregory got the pipe settled in the corner of his mouth and leaned a little further back in the chair and folded his hands over his stomach.

"Whaddya need?" he said.

"You remember Carmen Sternwood?" I said.

"The General's daughter," Gregory said without emotion, "the nympho."

"She was in a sanitarium," I said, "being treated, and she disappeared."

"Resthaven," Gregory said. "The butler called us."

"You looked into it?"

"I gave them a call," Gregory said.

"And?"

"And they say the butler is misinformed and there's no problem, and I ask to speak to her, and they say she's not well enough to speak to anyone, and I suggest we send a nurse over from the county health association to take a look at her, and they say that will not be acceptable and they hang up."

"Who'd you talk to?" I said.

"Guy in charge, Bonsentir."

"And you left it?" I said. "Just like that?"

"I called the sister, what's her name?"

"Vivian," I said.

"Right. The frail that's been toe dancing around town with Eddie Mars. I call her

50

and she says nothing to worry about. That she is not looking for her sister and feels that the butler was out of line calling us."

Gregory moved his hands from his stomach to lace them behind his head. He took in some smoke and blew it out easily around the pipestem in his mouth.

"And?" I said.

"And nothing. I got enough people that are actually missing to keep most of us pretty busy down here."

I couldn't see the sky outside Gregory's window. All I could see was a part of the hall of justice. As I stared out at it, a cloud must have floated past the sun, because a shadow fell on the building and then, almost as soon as it fell, it disappeared, and the hall was in sunshine again. Gregory sat in heavy silence while I observed this phenomenon. He was in no hurry. He had forever. Something would turn up.

I got a cigarette out and got it going and blew a little smoke at the window.

"Something wrong here," I said. "I know that most coppers aren't looking for a bigger caseload. But most coppers don't let some quack tell them to take the breeze either."

"What's your interest in this?" Gregory said.

"I'm looking for Carmen," I said.

"Got a client?"

"Norris," I said. "The butler."

"I figured Vivian fired him."

"I figure she can't," I said. "I figure the General left things that way."

"In the will," Gregory said.

"Sure."

Gregory nodded. He took the pipe out of his mouth and looked at the bowl and nodded again and put the pipe back in his mouth.

"Lot of different people are cops," Gregory said. "Some of them are better, some worse." He puffed some more smoke. "A lot of them are worse. But mostly, better or worse, when they do things that you don't expect them to do it's coming from above."

"Bonsentir's connected," I said.

Gregory shrugged. He took the pipe out of his mouth again, leaned forward slowly, and spat carefully into his wastebasket. Then he sat back slowly and just as carefully put the pipe back in his mouth.

"Bonsentir is a dead issue, Marlowe. He's fenced off, wrapped up. You can't get close enough to see him clearly."

"And if Carmen Sternwood is missing?" I said.

Gregory shrugged a slow shrug.

"Or in trouble?" I said.

"Marlowe, you're a big boy. I try to help

52

because last time we did business you played it pretty straight for a peeper, and Ohls in the sheriff's department says you're jake. But don't sit in my office and talk fairy tales we're both too old to believe in. If I tell you Claude Bonsentir has got juice, you can believe it. I'm not going to say this again, and outside this office I'll deny I said it. But you go up against Bonsentir you're a dead man, and I can't help you and Ohls can't help you."

I stood up.

"Nice talking to you, Captain," I said. "If Bonsentir calls, tell him I'm home filing the front sight on my machine gun."

Gregory didn't speak. He sat perfectly still, with a narrow blue ribbon of smoke wavering up from his pipe. I turned and went out and closed the door gently.

6

I still had my office that year in the Cahuenga
Building. I was in it with the windows open
and the hot Santa Ana wind pushing the
grit around on my desk top. I had the office
bottle of rye out and was having myself a
midday bracer while I let my feet dangle.
I was pretty sure Carmen was missing from
Bonsentir's sanitarium. And I was very sure
that everyone I talked with knew it, and
didn't want me to find her. What I couldn't
figure was why. Bonsentir might want to
cover up some incompetence and I figured
a guy like Bonsentir had a lot of things
under the covers up there that he might not
want the cops to start looking into. But why
would Vivian cover it up? And what kind
of clout did Bonsentir have that a good cop
like Gregory would walk away from it and
tell me to do the same? It was one thing
to buy off the local health inspector. Or the
local precinct captain, for that matter, but
when a downtown cop like Gregory said it
was locked up, that meant real juice and a
lot of it way up the line.

It meant that people whom Gregory would call "Sir" were on the payroll, and how much would that cost? How could Bonsentir have that kind of money? It made me tired to think about it, so I bought myself a second drink. Maybe it wasn't money. A guy like Bonsentir would know where there were bodies buried. That was how he flourished. I knew doctors like Bonsentir with the smooth faces and the radio voices. They had big sanitariums off somewhere, out of sight, where wealthy people could store their embarrassments: the dipsomaniac nephew, the nymphomaniac sister, the aging mother who liked to show her underwear, the eccentric brother-in-law who kept stealing things from Woolworth's. The wives of movie stars went to sanitariums like Resthaven, the sons of politicians went there. They were quiet.

Dr. Bonsentir had needles and pills and he used them. No one complained at Resthaven. Everyone smiled their gooney smiles and wandered about like sleepwalkers, and if they dreamed, who knew it, and who cared what they dreamed? Ah yes, good Doctor Bonsentir, I know you well.

I knew Dr. Bonsentir so well that I thought it best to toast him, so I poured out a last small splash of rye into the water glass I was using and sipped it in his honor. While

I was doing this I heard the door to my outer office open and close. There was silence then as if someone were standing out there trying to make up his mind. Or maybe as if someone were admiring my collection of ten-year-old *National Geographics*. Then the door opened and in came Vivian Sternwood in a polka-dot dress, big blue dots on a white background. Her hat and gloves were white and her big purse was the color of her dots.

"Care for a drink?" I said. "I was just toasting that great healer, Claude Bonsentir."

"You're drunk," she said.

"Probably not," I said. "But it's not to say I won't be."

I got up and went to the sink in the corner and got the other water glass I kept for company. I rinsed it, brought it back and poured a finger of rye into each glass.

I handed a glass to Vivian and while we stood I raised mine.

"I give you the Hippocrates of the quick needle, Dr. Bonsentir."

Vivian's eyes were bright with anger, but she drank a little rye.

"Are you going to ask me to sit down, Marlowe?"

"Certainly," I said. "Have a chair. Maybe we can have another toast, seated is okay, to the elusive Carmen Sternwood, whom no

56

one seems able to find but everybody says isn't missing."

"I know my sister is missing, Mr. Marlowe. I don't need some piece of drunken sarcasm from the likes of you."

"Who do you need it from," I said, "if not from me?"

"What I need from you is understanding. You must have some idea of what it is like to try and protect Carmen?"

"I have an idea what it's like to try to protect the rest of the world from Carmen," I said.

Vivian's face was dramatically hurt.

"I was hoping for better from you, Marlowe. I was hoping that the something that sparked between us before hasn't gone away completely."

I laughed and drank a little more of my rye.

"What went between us, Mrs. Regan, was you showing me your legs and trying to get me to do whatever you said because I'd seen your legs."

"And nothing more?"

I shrugged. Maybe there had been something more. I was after all getting drunk in the middle of the day.

"I don't know," I said. "Was there?"

"Yes," she said.

I wanted to believe her. Up close her eyes were nearly coal black and full of heat. She was wearing a lilac scent, an expensive one. And her wide mouth was soft looking with a full lower lip that seemed specifically meant to be nibbled on. I nodded and didn't say anything.

"I'm not as tough as I look, Marlowe," she said.

"If you were as tough as you look," I said, "you'd probably have to be licensed."

"I'm nowhere near as tough as you are," she said. "Oh, I know the smart mouth and the dark handsome looks and all of that. Just a lovable gumshoe. But I know what's inside that. I know that inside it's all iron and ice."

She leaned forward toward me, showing me a white lace bra and a good deal of breast as well. "But I'm betting that there's something else in there too."

"Don't bet your life on it, lady," I said. "I appreciate you showing me what you've got. But don't bet everything that you can melt the iron and ice."

She got up slowly and walked around the desk and sat quite carefully on my lap. She put her arms around my neck and leaned her face close to me. I could feel the heat of her breath on my face.

"Let's see," she said and pressed her mouth against mine, open. We explored that for a while, and when we finally broke, both of us were breathing harder than we had been. Vivian looked into my eyes from very close, so close that her eyes blurred as I'm sure mine must have to her.

"Maybe just a little melting?" she said.

"You found Carmen yet?" I said.

She stiffened and then stood up and walked back around the desk to her chair.

"Damn you," she said. "Goddamn you, Marlowe. Don't you change? Can't you ever change?"

Her voice shook a little and she had to look down and breathe a bit to get her composure. When she finally spoke her voice was a little hoarse.

"I know she's all right, Marlowe. I don't know where she is, but I know that Dr. Bonsentir knows and it's all right."

"That doesn't make any sense," I said.

"Please," she said. "You want to hear me beg, okay, listen. Please leave this alone. I know you don't care about money. But I'll pay you twice what Norris is paying, three times. If you will please just leave this alone."

"Have you spoken to Norris?" I said.

She shook her head.

"I cannot speak to Norris as I can speak to you."

"Why not," I said. "You could show him your legs. . . ." I finished it off with a hand flip.

"He's the butler, for God's sake, Marlowe. Do you enjoy humiliating me?"

"I'm not humiliating you," I said. "You're doing that yourself. I'm just after the truth."

"Truth," she said and laughed without even a hint of humor. "What the hell is the truth? And what difference does it ever make? You're like so many men. You have these things you think are so important. Truth. My Word. Honor. Right. Pride." She shook her head and laughed again. A laugh more painful than any scream. "You probably believe in love, for God's sake."

"What I believe in right now, Mrs. Regan, is finding Carmen."

"Why? In the name of God, why do you care? What difference can she ever make?"

"It's what I do for a living," I said. "Somebody hired me to do it."

"You will cause more trouble than you understand," Vivian said.

I didn't have anything to say to that, so I let it pass. We looked at each other for a while. Then Vivian sighed and stood up.

"I'm sorry, Marlowe," she said.

"Sure," I said. "I'm sorry too."

She turned and headed for the door. She opened it and turned for a moment and looked back as if she were going to say something. Then she shook her head and turned away.

"Vivian," I said.

She paused and looked back.

"I enjoyed the kiss," I said.

She stared at me for a moment and then shook her head again.

"That's the hell of it," she said. "I did too."

Then she turned and closed the door behind her. I sat and looked at it and sipped the rest of the rye. She must have left the outside door open. Because I didn't hear it close.

7

After Vivian left I corked the office bottle and put it back in the drawer. I went to the sink, rinsed out the glasses, washed my hands and face, and went back to my desk. I got out the phone book and looked up some numbers and made some calls. The L.A. County medical board had no registration of Dr. Claude Bonsentir.

The licensing board had never heard of him.

That taken care of, I went down on the boulevard and sat at a counter and had some late lunch. Never-at-a-loss Marlowe, the hungry detective. After lunch I strolled back up the boulevard toward my office. The movie executives were coming out of Musso & Frank's, telling each other how much they loved each other's last picture. The tourists walked along the sidewalk, heads down, staring at the stars in the pavement. If a real star had happened by they'd have never seen him. Near the Chinese theater a group of tourists stood and looked at the footprints in the concrete and listened to some sort of guide telling them about it. Outside the Roosevelt Hotel the prostitutes waited. They'd come from Keokuk and Great Falls, planning to start as starlets and become stars. It hadn't worked out. Some had started maybe as starlets, but they'd ended up as whores and as the afternoon began to wane, with its promise of evening, they gathered with the desperation in their eyes. Hollywood the town of sex and money and hokum for the tourists. A town where guys like Bonsentir could make a handsome living without a license, without any trace in the medical board records, without any interference from the buttons. Hooray.

Having been told by everyone but Daisy Duck to butt out, and having earned a total of one dollar on the case so far, the smart thing to do would have been to go back to the office and have another couple of pulls at my bottle of rye and think long thoughts about how glamorous it was to be in Hollywood. That being the smart thing to do, I got in my car and drove down to Las Olindas to see Eddie Mars. Which is how smart I am.

The Cypress Club was half hidden by a grove of wind-twisted cypress trees, which is probably why they called it the Cypress Club. It had once been a hotel and before that a rich man's house. It still looked like a rich man's house, grown a little shabby, and tarnished a bit by the beach fog that hung over it much of the time.

There was no doorman when I arrived, too early. The big double doors that separated the main room from the entry foyer were open. Inside there was only a barman setting up for the evening, and a Filipino in a white coat dry-mopping the old parquet floor. From somewhere in the dimness to my right a pasty-faced blond man appeared. He was slim and there was no expression in his face. I remembered him from when I first saw him in Arthur Gwynne Geiger's house with the smell of ether still in the air, and blood still on the rug.

If he remembered me he didn't show it.

"Place is closed for another couple of hours, bub."

"I know," I said. "I'm here to see Eddie."

"He know you're coming?"

"No."

"Then you probably aren't going to see him."

"It's the movies," I said. "All you hard guys think you have to act like some ham you saw in the movies. But he doesn't act that way because he's tough. He acts that way because he can't act. Go tell Eddie I'm here."

He gave me the same tough-guy blank

stare and turned and disappeared back into the gloom to the right. Pretty soon he came and said, "This way."

His expression hadn't changed. Nothing had changed. He acted like he didn't care about me. Maybe he wasn't acting.

Eddie Mars was still gray. Fine gray hair, gray eyes, neat gray eyebrows. His double-breasted flannel suit was gray, and his shirt was a lighter gray and his tie a darker gray except for two red diamonds in it. He had a hand in his coat pocket with the thumb out, the nail perfectly manicured, gleaming in the light from the big old bay window that looked out at the sea. The room was paneled, with a fabric frieze above the paneling. A wood fire burned in the deep stone fireplace and the smell of the woodsmoke mingled softly with the smell of the cold ocean. The time-lock safe was still in the corner. The Sèvres tea set still sat on its tray. It didn't look like it had been used any more than it had the last time I was here.

Mars grinned at me sociably. "Nice to see you again, soldier," he said.

"That's not what everybody else says."

Mars raised his even gray eyebrows. His face was tanned, and smooth-shaven, and healthy looking.

"People can be cruel," he said. "Any special

reason they're talking to you that way?"

"I keep asking them where Carmen Stern-wood is," I said.

Mars' face darkened. The smile stayed but it seemed less sociable.

"It's that kind of a visit, is it?" Mars said.

"Of course it is," I said. "Why would I come calling on you socially?"

"I thought we got along, Marlowe."

"You're a thug, Eddie. You look like a good polo player, and you've got a lot of money, and you know a lot of rich folks. But behind it you're a thug, and you've got goons like Blondie there to follow you around with a rod."

"And what's that to you?" Mars said. "Supposing what you say is true. What the hell are you? You're packing a rod, right now, under your left arm. You bend the law. You did it on Rusty Regan's death. The difference between me and you, soldier, is I make money and you don't."

"The difference between you and me, Eddie, is there's things I won't do."

Mars kept his smile and shrugged.

"What is it you wanted to ask me?" he said.

"What do you know about Carmen Stern-wood?"

Mars shrugged again. Distantly I could hear

the sound of the Pacific as it roiled against the foot of the cliff below the Cypress Club.

"Not much," he said. "Except what you know."

"You know where she is now?"

Mars shook his head. "Last I knew she was in a sanitarium up the top of Coldwater Canyon."

"She's not there now," I said.

"She run off?"

It was my turn to shrug.

"Vivian hire you?" Mars said.

"No," I said. "She's one of the people telling me to butt out."

"Lot of hard edge to that woman," Mars said.

"She also told me that you had promised her you'd find Carmen."

Mars was silent a moment. Then he said, "That a fact?"

"What she said," I answered.

"Why would I do that?" Mars said.

"Same reason you rigged it to look like Rusty Regan ran off with your wife," I said. " 'Cause you're sweet."

Mars laughed out loud.

"Sweet," he said. "Soldier, I've got to say I always enjoy you."

"Like you enjoyed me when I found your wife and Regan wasn't with her. And you were afraid I'd blow the whistle that maybe Regan really was dead. Like you enjoyed me when you told Lash Canino to kill me?"

Mars shrugged. "I underestimated you, soldier. How'd you take Canino anyway?"

"Your wife helped me. Mona Mars in the silver wig."

"Ex-wife," Mars said.

"Canino's car was parked outside the farmhouse in Rialto," I said. "Empty. And I was behind it wearing handcuffs, but I had a gun. And big brave Lash came out to get me, pushing your wife in front of him."

She came down the steps. Now I could see the white stiffness of her face. She started toward the car. A bulwark of defense for Canino, in case I could still spit in his eye. Her voice spoke through the lisp of the rain, saying slowly, without any tone: "I can't see a thing, Lash. The windows are misted."

He grunted something and the girl's body jerked hard, as though he had jammed a gun into her back. She came on again and drew near the lightless car. I could see him behind her now, his hat, a side of his face, the bulk of his shoulder. The girl stopped rigid and screamed. A beautiful thin tearing scream that rocked me like a left hook.

"I can see him!" she screamed. "Through

the window. Behind the wheel, Lash!"

He fell for it like a bucket of lead. He knocked her roughly to one side and jumped forward, throwing his hand up. Three more spurts of flame cut the darkness. More glass scarred. One bullet went on through and smacked a tree on my side. A ricochet whined off into the distance. But the motor went quietly on.

He was low down, crouched against the gloom, his face a grayness without form that seemed to come back slowly after the glare of the shots. If it was a revolver he had, it might be empty. It might not. He had fired six times, but he might have reloaded inside the house. I hoped he had. I didn't want him with an empty gun. But it might be an automatic.

I said: "Finished?"

He whirled at me. Perhaps it would have been nice to allow him another shot or two, just like a gentleman of the old school. But his gun was still up and I couldn't wait any longer. Not long enough to be a gentleman of the old school. I shot him four times, the Colt straining against my ribs. The gun jumped out of his hands as if it had been kicked. He reached both his hands for his stomach. I could hear them smack hard against his body. He fell like that,

69

straight forward, holding himself together with his broad hands. He fell facedown in the wet gravel. And after that there wasn't a sound from him. . . .

"You ever see her, Eddie?"

Mars shook his head. "Not since the night I sprang her from the DA's living room," he said. "I took her home and went to make a drink and when I came back she was gone."

"So you divorced her."

"Uh huh."

"And turned for solace to Vivian Regan."

"You think so?"

"I got the impression you and she might be sort of an item," I said.

"And if we were?"

"Then you might be sweet enough to find her little sister for her."

"Those frails are poison, Marlowe. The younger one's sicker than a week-old oyster, and Vivian's the kind of broad that will always drive too fast. She breaks things."

"But there's all that money," I said.

"Never mind that maybe I should take offense that I'd chase one of these broads to marry into the mashed potatoes," Mars said. "The thing is, I don't need it. I got enough."

"Enough doesn't mean anything to guys

70

like you, Eddie."

Mars' smile vanished, and his face showed suddenly just how hard a guy he was.

"You don't want to get in my way, soldier, unless you like the idea of breathing through your navel."

"Lash Canino couldn't do it, Eddie."

Mars pointed at me with the forefinger of his right hand and then swiveled his wrist and pointed toward the door.

"You're on your way, soldier," he said. "But while you're leaving think about something. I got no reason to care about what happens to you, and no reason to lie to you; but I'm telling you" — Mars' face broke into a grin — "because I'm sweet, that if people are telling you to stay out of the Carmen Sternwood deal, and to stay away from that sanitarium where they stashed her, then do it. You'll regret it if you don't."

The grin had disappeared by the time he finished.

I moved toward the door.

"See you around," I said. "If somebody hasn't scared me to death in the meantime."

I closed the door and left, and drove back to Hollywood knowing every bit as much as I'd known when I drove down.

Which was nothing at all.

8

The canyon where Resthaven nestled ran back along the hill for a ways, and the road on which Resthaven fronted followed the canyon and looped up and behind the sanitarium before it trailed back out onto Coldwater again. I parked my car on Coldwater Canyon under an olive tree. The morning was bright and still. It would be a hot day, but it wasn't hot yet and everything still looked unwilted. There was dust on the leaves of the olive tree, and the small black fruit that had fallen from the tree crunched underfoot when I got out of the car. The traffic on Coldwater Canyon Drive was heading both ways over the hill to work. I walked around behind Resthaven and up the side loop that put me on the canyon, looking down at the sanitarium. In Beverly Hills Oriental servants were squeezing orange juice and people in silk robes were eating soft-boiled eggs in little egg cups and glancing through the morning paper. But here, behind the screen of scrub growth along the rim of the canyon, I couldn't see the L.A. basin. I could have been in Fargo or Bellows Falls except for the heat and the dryness. I looked down at Resthaven Sanitarium.

It was a large sweep of green lawn which ended at the foot of the canyon wall on which I stood. The wall formed a natural barrier. The other end of the lawn abutted the central house and an eight-foot-high brick wall ran from either end of the house to the foot of the canyon. There were shrubs along the walls, and flowering jacaranda which made it look ornamental, but it would take an agile patient to get over it. There was a pool with red stone terracing around it, and near the canyon wall, a croquet lawn where several men and women played a morning round. The players were dressed variously. Some in what seemed to be a hospital uniform of black linen pajamas and sandals, but two of the men were in suits and ties, and one woman was in evening dress.

The beachboy I'd seen earlier was lounging on a chaise near the pool, watching the patients and working on his tan. The Mexican was nowhere in sight, nor was Dr. Bonsentir. I squatted on my haunches at the rim of the canyon, hidden by some scrub oak, and observed. The croquet proceeded languidly, and as the sun got higher and burned away the last wisp of night coolness, the beachboy shifted his chaise into the shade of a big beach umbrella. He was reading the paper and periodically glancing at his charges. After a while he lay back in the chaise and, with the paper draped over his face, lay perfectly still. There wouldn't be a better time. I went over the rim of the canyon.

It was nearly vertical but scattered with scrub pine and oak and juniper and I was able to slide down from handhold to handhold and drop into the croquet lawn without collecting more dirt than would grow an acre of spinach. If the players thought there was anything odd about someone sliding down the canyon into their game they didn't do anything to suggest it. In fact they paid me no attention as they went about tapping the wooden balls with their mallets and with subdued pleasure sending their opponent's ball away from the wicket. The beachboy never stirred.

There was something odd about this croquet game. It took me a minute to realize what it was as I shook the stones and assorted gravel out of my shirt. No one spoke. The game proceeded in complete silence except for the click of the ball and the occasional pleased chuckle. The woman in the evening gown played in long gloves and high slingstrap silver slippers. One of the men had on a pale tan suit with a thin cream pinstripe in it. He wore a cream-colored linen vest and light tan shoes. His bright green silk tie was tied in a wide Windsor knot. They were all doped to the eyeballs and were playing their game to a tune I couldn't hear.

Walking softly on the grass, I went past the sleeping attendant and in through a back door into the same long low ranch-style main building that I'd been in before. It was cool inside, and dim. I was in a game room. There were two billiards tables and a Ping-Pong table. Along one wall there were card tables set up and across the back wall was a low counter with stools where maybe milk and cookies was served, or maybe opium and a flagon of ether.

To the left a long corridor ran down the back side of the long house. I went down that way. The left-hand wall was punctuated with doors and each door led into a patient's room. The first one was empty. In the second room was a wispy old lady wearing a flowered nightdress with a lace collar. Her gray hair framed her face in soft permanent waves. There was the hint of a beautiful youth about her. It whispered in the way she held her head and the repose of her small body in the chair. She had a large picture book open on her lap and she was looking at it intently through gold-rimmed wire glasses. I stepped quietly into the room. On the half-open door was a small plate that said MRS. NORMAN SWAYZE.

"Good morning, Mrs. Swayze," I said.

She looked up from her book and smiled at me.

"Hi," she said.

"I'm Dr. Marlowe," I said. "How are you feeling this morning?"

I closed the door quietly behind me as I spoke.

"Oh, I'm perfectly fine, doctor," she said. "This morning I was looking out the window trying to see my house, but I don't think I can see it. Can you?"

"Where do you live, Mrs. Swayze?"

She pointed toward the window.

"Over there," she said brightly, "somewhere."

I nodded and glanced out the window.

"No," I said. "I don't see your house either."

"I look," she said. "I look all the time, but I never seem able to find it."

As I got closer I could see that her book was a high-class, well-printed four-color collection of some of the filthiest pornographic photographs I had ever seen. It was the kind of expensive smut that Arthur Gwynne Geiger had peddled out of his shop on Hollywood Boulevard near Las Palmas. But that was a while ago now, before I killed Lash Canino.

The old lady had lost interest in me and was studying her book again, licking her thumb periodically to turn a page. Hunched over the big book in her small lap, she looked like a gentle sparrow. On the bureau against the wall, and piled on the nightstand beside her bed, were other books just like the one she had, well bound, well produced, and filthier than a Tijuana latrine.

She looked up and saw me looking at the books.

"Would you like to read one of my books?" she said. "I love books like this. Do you?"

I shook my head. "No, ma'am," I said. "Not exactly."

"Well, I do," she said firmly. "And the doctor gets them for me anytime I want them."

"Dr. Bonsentir?" I said.

"Yes — well, not himself always, sometimes one of the young men gets them for me."

"Mrs. Swayze," I said, "do you know Carmen Sternwood?"

She let the book rest open in her lap. There were two women and a man in a double-truck full-color spread. I tried not to notice.

"Carmen?" she said. She had straightened and her forehead wrinkled slightly as she tried to pull the raveled threads of her aging mind together.

"Carmen Sternwood," I said. "Young woman, smallish, nice figure, light brown hair. Her thumbs were sort of odd-looking."

Mrs. Swayze smiled. It was the thumbs.

"Of course. Carmen. She lives here too. Yes. She often comes in to read my books. Sometimes we read them together."

"Have you seen her lately?" I said.

Mrs. Swayze's face tightened a little. It made her cheeks pinch and redden.

"I think she went off with Mr. Simpson. I think she's visiting him."

"Really?" I said. "Do you know Mr. Simpson's full name?"

Mrs. Swayze's eyes got very wide and she looked a little frightened.

"Me? I don't know. I don't know anyone's first name. I don't remember very much anymore. I can't even remember where my house is. I look and I look and I can't see it."

"Do you know where Mr. Simpson's house is?"

She shook her head vigorously, and pointed again, vaguely, toward the window.

"Over there," she said, "I imagine."

"Do you know why she went to visit Mr. Simpson?" I said.

Mrs. Swayze smiled secretively and winked at me.

"A lot of the young girls here go to visit Mr. Simpson."

"Do they usually come back?"

"I don't know," she said. Her tone suggested that the question was idiotic.

Then her eyes shifted past me and she said, "Hi, sweetie."

I turned. Sweetie was the Mexican, on crepe-soled shoes, who had opened the door behind me. I should have smelled him. He was rank as a goat. His small eyes fixed on me and never left.

"I've been talking with Dr. Marlowe," Mrs. Swayze said. "He tried to see my house for me but he says he can't."

The Mexican's eyes never wavered.

"*Sí*, Señora Swayze," he said. Then he raised a forefinger and curled it toward him and gestured me toward the hall. I turned to Mrs. Swayze and bowed slightly.

"If I see your house," I said, "I'll let you know."

As I said it I slipped my gun out from under my arm and held it down against my leg, where the Mexican couldn't see it. Then

79

I straightened and turned to leave.

"Thank you, doctor," Mrs. Swayze said. She was bent back over her book, fully engrossed again, wetting her thumb to turn the next page.

The Mexican backed out of the room ahead of me and as I reached the hall and stepped away from the door he whistled a punch with his left hand that caught me on the side of the jaw and slammed me back against the wall. It was like being hit by a bowling ball. I banged into the wall, my legs felt rubbery and I slid a little downward, trying to brace against the wall with my back as I slid. There was no expression on the Mexican's face as he stepped in to me and rammed his forearm up under my chin, and pinned me back against the wall. His breath was sour in my face as he came in against me and I saw his eyes suddenly widen as I jammed the muzzle of the Colt into his belly under his rib cage.

"Back up," I said hoarsely, "your breath is wilting my suit."

The Mexican stepped back carefully and stood with his hands a little away from his sides, his small eyes still steady on me.

"Now," I said, "you and I are going to walk down this corridor and into the front hall and out the front door. And you're going to do it backwards."

He made no motion, he said nothing. I could feel the tension in him, like a trigger waiting to be pulled. I hoped he could feel the same thing in me. Especially because I had a trigger to pull.

"Move," I said.

He backed slowly down the corridor, moving through the patches of sunlight where the doors to patients' rooms were open and the light streamed in from the east. Dust motes lazed in the sunlight. At the far end of the corridor there was a door in the right wall. I jerked the gun at it and it opened and we were in the entry hall where I'd waited to see Dr. Bonsentir. The slick-haired man in the white coat was there. He looked at me and made a move with his hand. I shook my head and he froze.

"You too," I said. "Both of you face the wall, hands on the wall, spread your legs, back away from the wall so the weight is on your hands."

They did as they were told. No one spoke. I patted them down. The Mexican had no gun. He'd probably gotten hungry one day and eaten it. I took a Smith and Wesson .38 out from under the other guy's left arm.

"Anyone pokes his nose through the door," I said, "gets a bullet in it."

No one moved or spoke. I opened the front door carefully and looked out. The front yard was empty. The two orderlies leaned on the wall. I stepped out the front door and closed it and ran for my car.

9

There were 105 people named Simpson in the L.A. phone book, if you counted the guy who spelled it without the P, or the one who spelled it Sympson. Of them, five were women, and three more had only the first initial and thus probably were women. Which left only 97 people for me to run down. If Carmen was with someone whose phone was listed, or with someone in L.A. If his real name was Mr. Simpson. My source was not impeccable.

I got up from my desk and stared out the window at the heat shimmering up off Hollywood Boulevard. The sun was steady and hot, and the smell of the grill from the coffee shop downstairs went perfectly with the weather. My coat was off and hanging on my chair. My shirt stuck to my back and I had taken off my shoulder holster and hung it on the chair over my coat, handy in case a horde of sanitarium orderlies burst in and tried to stick me in a straitjacket. If I looked left I could stare down Cahuenga toward lower Hollywood, out of the glitter district where big comfortable homes with deep verandas still lined quiet streets. It would be cool inside those homes with their thick walls and their low roofs, some people kept the windows closed and the heat out, others opened them for ventilation and the lace curtains would stir lazily in the hot wind and make a soft whisper. But listen though I might, it didn't whisper where Carmen Sternwood was. I needed a different approach.

I called Vivian Regan. Her maid said she was resting. I said I'd be there in an hour. I washed my hands and face in the sink. Dried them, put my shoulder holster back on and my coat and went down to get my car. I drove over the Alta Brea Crescent with the top down and the hot wind blew some of the perspiration off my face. But my shirt was still wet under my jacket and my hat band was damp. I was early to the Sternwoods' so I cruised a little in the hills, looking at all the sprinklers on all the lawns. Brown was the normal and permanent color of southern California, it was held at bay by regiments of lawn sprinklers.

At two I was at the front door of the Sternwood home. The maid opened the door for me and led me through the house to the patio beside the pool where Vivian lay on a pink chaise under a pink and white umbrella, wearing a gleaming white one-piece swimsuit. She had on oversized sunglasses and there was an ice bucket handy with a bottle of champagne in it. Vivian's body was tanned the color of honey and all of it that I could see was smooth and resilient.

"My God, Marlowe," she said to me. "Take off your coat in this beastly heat."

"I'm wearing a gun," I said.

"For goodness' sake I should hope so," Vivian said. "I don't mind. I might rather like to see it, actually."

I peeled my jacket off and folded it and put it on the ground. I took the chair she offered and tilted my hat brim forward so that the sun would stay out of my eyes.

"Would you care for champagne?" Vivian said. "On a day like this I find it helps take your mind off the heat."

She took a sip of her champagne from a fluted glass.

Moisture had beaded on the side of the ice bucket and coursed down along the sides, making fine tracks in the condensation.

"When I drink champagne in the sun," I said, "I get a walloping headache."

"Well" — she laughed, showing teeth perfectly even and perfectly white — "why not get over here under the umbrella?"

She poured some champagne and handed it to me. I took it and turned the glass slowly in my hands. I watched her face closely.

"Know anyone named Simpson?" I said.

She didn't choke on the champagne, but it was only ten generations of iron breeding that saved her. For a moment her face fell apart, and then she got it back together again and said very casually, "No, I don't believe I do."

I nodded, as if I believed her.

"Why do you ask?" she said even more casually than she had spoken before.

"I have information that Carmen may be with him."

Vivian drank some champagne, maybe a little more quickly than she had previously.

"What was the name?" she said as if she were asking the time of day.

"Simpson," I said.

Vivian shook her head vaguely and patted the upholstered chaise beside her.

"Come and sit over here and stop sweating so much," she said.

I got up and moved into the shade and sat on the chaise. Vivian poured more champagne into my glass and some into hers. She drank. With one bright red fingernail she traced the outlines of my gun in its holster.

"Frightening things," she said. "But somehow fascinating."

She moved the tracing finger up from the gun, along my shoulder line and along the edge of my jaw.

"Like you," she said, "a dark deadly brute of a thing."

"You should see me in my teal robe," I said.

Her lipstick was brilliant red and made a wide bright slash across her evenly tanned face. Her black eyes seemed hotter at close range. She rolled onto her side and put her arms around me. The champagne glass had disappeared somewhere on her side of the chaise. She slid her hands up my back and riffled the hair at the back of my neck. We were pressed together from knee to forehead.

"There's not much between us," she said with her lips fluttering against mine as she spoke.

"In a manner of speaking," I said. I was doing everything I could not to whinny like a stallion.

"Just a thin layer of bathing suit," she whispered, "that zips down the back."

I slid my hand down the line of her zipper. She arched her body hard against me and pressed her mouth against mine. We hung that way, balanced on the edge of the chaise, and of God knows what else. Finally she pulled her head back. Her lipstick was smeared.

"The zipper." Her voice was hoarse.

I shook my head.

"Not like this," I said. "Like a clotheshorse towel boy on the chaise by the pool. Do I get a tip afterwards?"

Her eyes widened.

"You don't want me?" she said.

"I want you, but when it's me and you, not you trying to distract me so I won't keep asking about a guy named Simpson who may have your baby sister."

Tears welled into her eyes. We were both sitting up on the chaise now, though in truth I couldn't remember changing position. Her fists clenched.

"You terrible son of a bitch, Marlowe. You arrogant bastard. My baby sister. God, how can you know. How can you even imagine what it's like to have to be in charge of that baby sister?"

"I've had a taste of it," I said.

"A taste. I've had a lifetime. And now I have her alone. My father's gone, which is just as well. She would break his heart if he were here."

"Or she were," I said.

Vivian seemed to be really crying now.

"You don't know, Marlowe, what it is like, a woman alone, trying to manage Carmen, trying to keep the General's memory so that his name isn't dishonored, so that he can sleep in peace."

"When I mentioned Simpson," I said, "you acted like you'd swallowed a mouse."

Vivian put her face in her hands and began to sob, her honey-colored shoulders hunched. Her whole body shook with the crying.

"Damn you, Marlowe, why can't you leave me alone?"

"I'm a detective, lady. I work at it. I've got a client. He deserves my best effort."

Without looking up, her face still pressed into her hands, she said, "The only Simpson I know is Randolph Simpson."

"Is Carmen with him?" I said.

"I don't know."

"Where does he live?"

"Above Malibu," she said. "In the hills."

"Thanks," I said. "For the champagne too."

"He's too much for you, Marlowe. You can't go against him."

"I've heard that before," I said. "I'm still around."

She shook her head in her hands.

I couldn't think of anything else to say so I gave her the gunman's salute with my forefinger and turned and walked away.

Behind me I heard her call me a bastard. A lot of people had called me that. Could all of them be wrong?

10

There was no Randolph Simpson in the phone book. I went down to the library and looked in the collection of street directories. No listing. I went over to the hall of records and began digging through the real estate tax rolls, and after three very dusty hours I found him. Randolph Simpson, Sierra Verdugo Rd. I went back to my office and looked at my map. Sierra Verdugo Rd. was in the Santa Monica Mountains, west of Topanga Canyon and south of Mulholland. A guy that lived there and kept his name out of the city directory and had his phone number unlisted probably didn't welcome a visit from a stranger.

I put on my hat and went to my car and drove right out to see him.

Sierra Verdugo Rd. cut through the parched hills that people out here called mountains between the Pacific Coast Highway and the San Fernando Valley.

They still shot Westerns out here, low-budget stuff with aging stars on tired horses, and as I wound through the narrow turns of the road I half expected to see a band of rampaging Indians round the bend. The hills were brown and barren except for the scrubby low growth of indeterminate species that clung to the otherwise eroding hillsides. Boulders the size of outhouses teetered near the rim of the highway, looking as if you could reach out as you drove by and push them over into the canyon. The road west off Topanga Canyon went slowly upward in a series of S turns until it widened into a graded turnaround in front of a large iron gate. The gate was set into a ten-foot fieldstone and mortar wall that circled slowly out of sight in both directions. The wall was topped with broken glass of many colors set sharply in the mortar. Beyond the gate was a plain of green grass highlighted with flower beds and flowering shrubs. In the middle of the sere hills it looked like a vision of Eden from the plains to the east.

I parked my car near the gate and got out and walked to it. Beyond the gate was a small guard shack that looked like a miniature castle. A man came out and walked to the gate. He looked like a tough accountant. Dark suit, white shirt, dark tie, sunglasses.

"What can I do for you?" he said. His hair was cut short and very neatly trimmed around the ears.

"Looking for Randolph Simpson," I said.

He smiled politely and nodded encouragingly.

"I had the impression he lived here," I said.

"Really," he said.

"I wish to talk with him about Carmen Sternwood."

"I'm afraid you've made a mistake, sir," he said.

"Sure," I said. "I'd drive all the way up here without knowing that Simpson lived here. In fact I just drive around L.A. in my spare time knocking on doors at random and asking for Randolph Simpson."

The gate guard smiled as politely as a tax collector, but not as warmly.

"Mr. Simpson doesn't accept callers," he said.

"He might make an exception for me," I said. "Call the house, check it out. Tell him it's Marlowe about Carmen Sternwood."

The guard looked silently at me for a moment. Hard to be sure. I could be important, and it could be that turning me away without checking would get him in trouble. Maybe Carmen Sternwood was important. He made up his mind.

"Wait here, please," he said, and went back into the little guard castle.

He was gone maybe five minutes and when

he came out another guard came with him. The other guard was dressed the same, including the sunglasses, but he was nearly bald and what hair he had left he'd plastered in wispy strips across the otherwise hairless skin of his head.

"Step out of the car, please," the first guard said. "Place your hands on the roof."

I did and the bald guard patted me down and took my gun from under my left arm.

"Calling card?" he said.

"You never know," I said. "I've heard they have jackrabbits up here as big as bears. There's ID in my wallet."

"I was getting to that," the bald guard said.

He looked at the photostat of my license in the glassine window of my wallet.

"Private creeper," he said to his partner, "outta Hollywood."

His partner nodded, looked at the wallet and passed it back to me.

"Follow the drive," he said. "Don't stop the car. Don't get out. Somebody will meet you at the front door." He dropped my gun in the side pocket of his dark suit coat.

"We'll hold the rod till you come down," he said. "So you don't hurt yourself."

I got back in my car and cranked the starter. The big gates swung slowly back and I drove slowly through them. Inside it was greener and brighter than a movie star's dreams. There were fountains and flowers in profusion and the grass under the steady arc of the sprinklers gleamed like the top of a pool table under the unwavering southern California sun. The drive was done in some kind of crushed shell, and curved, white and still, through the intense landscape until it reached the main building. The place looked like a Moorish fortress in a pale gray stucco with turrets on the corners and gunports every few feet across the top.

Another guy in a dark suit and hard face opened the door for me and turned me over to a Chinese houseman who led me through a series of darkly paneled rooms to a long room with a gas fire in the oversized, tile-inlaid fireplace. In a huge oak chair with elaborately carved arms a woman sat, with her hands folded in her lap. She had steel-gray hair, and eyes to match.

"I'm Jean Rudnick," she said. "Kindly tell me the purpose of your visit."

She was wearing a mannish gray suit with a pinstripe, and a white shirt and a little gray and white striped tie. Her nails were painted lavender, and her gold-rimmed glasses enlarged her eyes so that they dominated her face.

"My name is Philip Marlowe," I said. "I'm a private detective and I've been hired to find Carmen Sternwood, who is missing from a sanitarium in Beverly Hills."

"And why do you wish to see Mr. Simpson?" she said.

"I have information that Carmen's here."

"From whom?"

I shook my head. "Sorry," I said.

"Mr. Marlowe," she said and her voice was full of the tiredness and superiority that people's voices get full of when they have too much power and wield it much too often, "I don't know if you know who I am, but I am Mr. Simpson's personal assistant and if someone is making ludicrous charges involving some girl and Mr. Simpson, then I must insist on knowing who that person is."

"How'd you know Carmen is a girl?" I said.

"I beg your pardon?"

"You said charges involving Mr. Simpson and some girl. Why do you think it's a girl? There's lots of men named Carmen. Carmen Lombardo, Carmen Cavallaro, Carmen . . ."

"Mr. Marlowe, please, I have no time for cheap parlor games."

"Then don't play them with me, Miss Rudnick."

"Mrs."

"My congratulations to Mr.," I said.

"Mr. Rudnick is deceased," she said. "Are you actually aware of who Mr. Simpson is?"

"Looking around," I said, "I'd guess he was Ali Baba."

"My God — how stupid can you be. You are entirely over your head and you haven't any idea. You really don't know."

"Yeah," I said. "Sometimes I weep softly into my pillow just thinking about it. How about Simpson, do I see him?"

"Certainly not," Mrs. Rudnick said. The thought seemed to cause her chest pains.

"Does Simpson know anyone named Sternwood?" I said.

"He certainly does not," Mrs. Rudnick said. Throughout our conversation she sat perfectly still with her hands folded in her lap, like a picture of Queen Victoria.

"Maybe he knows them and hasn't told you," I said.

That seemed to give her more chest pains.

"Mr. Marlowe," she said, "I am Mr. Simpson's *personal* assistant! I have the pleasure of his full confidence. If he knew anyone named Sternwood, I too would know of it."

"Vivian Sternwood knows him," I said.

"Mr. Marlowe, I'm afraid this conversation is at an end."

She picked up a small brass bell on the

side table and jingled it discreetly.

The door behind me opened and two of the suits came through it.

"I want you to pay attention to me," Mrs. Rudnick said, "and not dismiss what I tell you simply because I am a woman. If you persist in annoying Mr. Simpson on this, or *any* matter, you will regret it for whatever is left of your life."

"I'm not dismissing it because you're a woman, Mrs. Rudnick," I said. "I'm dismissing it because it doesn't scare me. The boys in the dark suits don't scare me. Randolph Simpson, whoever the hell he is, doesn't scare me. And if you think I've been annoying so far, wait until I shift into third."

"You've been warned, Mr. Marlowe," Jean Rudnick said coldly. Her hands were still folded in her lap and her steely eyes never blinked as she watched me leave.

The two suits walked me to my car and stood looking at me blankly as I got in.

I started up and let out the clutch and started down the driveway. As I left, I thought, for a moment, that I saw something stir in a second-floor window, a face for only a moment, then nothing. I drove on down the curving roadway and out through the ornate iron gate that closed silently behind me.

11

Captain Gregory gazed sadly at me across his desk and slowly shook his head.

"You got a better chance of getting a search warrant for the White House," Gregory said. "I told you Bonsentir was wired. Simpson's who he's wired to."

"Just because he's got a hundred million dollars?"

"Just because of that," Gregory said. "I know it shouldn't be that way, and you know it shouldn't be that way, but you and I both been around too long to think it won't be that way here in the good old USA."

"Even though I have reason to believe that there's a missing girl there, maybe a kidnap victim?"

"You got the word of one wappy old dame in a sanitarium who spends her time reading stuff would make me blush."

"And Mrs. Rudnick's denial that she'd ever heard of the Sternwoods?"

"Maybe she hasn't. Maybe she doesn't know everyone her boss knows. Maybe Vivian knows him and he don't know her. Just because she knows him don't mean he's got her sister."

"Be a pretty fair-sized coincidence," I said. "The old lady in Resthaven tells me Carmen's with a guy named Simpson, and Vivian knows a guy named Simpson."

"Sure," Gregory said. "I don't like coincidence either. In the cop business you learn to doubt it. But it happens. And even if you and me and the mayor all saw her there, you still don't get a search warrant in this county to go through Randolph Simpson's house."

"He buy a piece of you too, Captain?" I said.

Gregory shifted comfortably in his chair and fumbled in his coat for pipe and tobacco.

"Sure," he said. "I'm just a dumb crooked copper. Everybody buys me. I got it coming in in grocery sacks. Which is why I'm driving a ten-year-old heap and living in a house too small and take the old lady out, maybe once a month, for an enchilada and a small beer."

"Forget I said that," I said.

"I try and stay reasonably honest, Marlowe. And I try to do my job. But I got a kid to put through college and I got retirement pay to think about. I do what I can."

"Sure," I said.

"You're not going to leave this alone,

are you, Marlowe?"

"It's how I make my living, Captain. People hire me to do stuff that the cops don't or won't do. It doesn't help my career to leave things unfinished. All I got to sell is that I'll stick to something, that I'll take it to the end, you know?"

Gregory nodded. He had the pipe filled and was lighting it as carefully as he always did everything. As if it were the most important thing he would do that day, maybe ever.

"Where I can help you, son, I will. But don't look for much."

"I never have, Captain."

Gregory nodded again, and took in a lot of pipe smoke and let it out in a slow reflective cloud that hung in the air between us. He put up a thick hand and waved it gently to dispel the smoke.

"You got any next of kin?" he said.

"No," I said. "Anything you care to tell me about Simpson except how rich he is?"

"Nope," Gregory said. "You know more than you ought to now."

"Thanks for the encouragement, Captain. I hope you enjoy your pension."

"Hit the road, Marlowe," Gregory said. "I'm tired of talking with you."

"Sorry to disturb your nap," I said and

turned and left the office.

Outside the heat shimmered up off the pavement like a mirage. The tar on the streets was soft from it. I drove back out Sunset to Hollywood with the top down and the hot wind in my face.

12

It was hot. I had the window open in my office but all that did was let me know that it was just as hot outside. The heat made everything still. There was little traffic on the boulevard, and what people there were walked slowly and stayed in the hot shade whenever they could find any. The sky was cloudless and bluer than cornflowers. I had my coat and vest off, and every little while I'd go to the sink in the corner and rinse my face and neck with tepid water from the tap.

It was the kind of heat where families begin to eye each other's throats, where mousy accountants turn savagely on their boss, where irritation turns to anger and anger turns to murder, and murder turns into rampage.

The phone rang. It was Bernie Ohls, the DA's chief investigator.

"Got a murder off Beverly Glen," he said. "Near Stone Canyon Reservoir. Thought you might want to ride out with me and take a look."

"Better than sitting here in a slow oven," I said.

I was outside on the corner of Cahuenga when Ohls came by ten minutes later. He didn't seem in a hurry. He didn't hit the siren as we rolled down the boulevard west, toward Beverly Glen.

Ohls was a medium-sized guy, blondish hair, stiff white eyebrows. He had nice even teeth and calm eyes and looked like most other medium-sized guys, except that I knew he had killed at least nine men, three when somebody thought he'd been covered. He was smoking a little cigar.

"Found several pieces of a woman, in a gully off the Glen, down maybe a hundred yards from the road. There wasn't much blood and there were several parts missing, so it looks like she was dismembered somewhere else and dumped there." Ohls puffed a bit of smoke and the hot air swirled it out the open window. "Since not all of her is there, we figure she was probably dumped elsewhere too."

I felt the pull of gravity at the bottom of my stomach.

"You ID'd her yet?" I said.

"Not really," Ohls said. "Her head's missing and both hands."

We slid down Fairfax and onto Sunset.

"So why'd you invite me along? You miss me?"

"I heard you were looking for Carmen Sternwood," Ohls said.

The weight at the bottom of my stomach got heavier.

"Un huh."

"There was a purse with the body. All the ID was out of it, but whoever did it missed a book of matches. Inside the matches was a phone number."

"Carmen's?" I said.

Ohls nodded.

"One of the harness boys called and checked as soon as they found it."

"I thought they were supposed to leave that to the detectives," I said.

Ohls grinned. "Guy's planning to be chief," he said.

Near the top of Beverly Glen, before you make the curve to Mulholland Drive, there were four black and white L.A. police cars, and two L.A. sheriff's cars. Behind them was an ambulance with its back doors open, and an L.A. County fire rescue truck with its light still rotating. Ohls pulled in behind the ambulance and flashed his badge to the sweating uniform cop directing traffic. Then he and I scrambled on down the embankment, through the scrub pine and interlacing thorny vines that grew among them. There was the hot smell of vegetation and old pine needles and the harsher smell of fallen eucalyptus leaves. The slope flattened into a gully and in the gully were half a dozen assorted county employees including a man from the coroner's office with a white coat on over his tie and vest. He was a fat guy with a neck that spilled out over his collar and his face was bright red as he straightened from squatting next to a tarpaulin-covered form.

He knew Ohls.

"This is a real mess, Lieutenant," he said. He shook his head in disgust and slowly peeled back the tarp by one corner. "Guy didn't even have sharp tools," he said.

Under the tarp was the bottom half of a woman's torso, with one leg attached.

Ohls had no reaction.

The medical examiner draped the tarpaulin back over the corpse.

"There's couple other parts," he said, "over here." He nodded his head toward another tarp. "We let everything lie where we found it."

"Wonderful," Ohls said.

"Want to take a look?"

"Not right now," Ohls said. "You know anything?"

"Woman's dead," the medical examiner said.

"Always brightens up a case," Ohls said, "to have a funny ME."

The medical examiner chuckled so that the fat on his neck wobbled a little over his collar.

"Don't know a hell of a lot more than that, yet."

"Cause of death?" Ohls said. "Aside from getting cut up like a fryer?"

"No way to know until we find all the pieces," the medical examiner said. "Don't know if she was alive when she was cut up."

Ohls shook his head harshly as if there was a bee in his ear.

"ID?" he said.

"Caucasian, female, judging from what we've got, not an old woman. Twenties or thirties, maybe a well-preserved forty at the oldest. Skin tone is still pretty good, what there is of it."

"Any idea yet when?"

The medical examiner shook his head.

"Last couple days at the outside, assuming she was dumped here shortly after she was killed, and wasn't refrigerated someplace. That's as close as I can get." He glanced down at the tarpaulin heap in front of him. "We've got a stomach, at least, so we can make some guesses depending on when she ate, and what she ate, but we're not going to get much closer. Blood's all drained out of her. That screws us up."

"What a shame," Ohls said. "Any thoughts, Marlowe? Could be the Sternwood girl."

"Guess on the skin coloration?" I said.

The medical examiner reached down. "I'd say dark. Here, take a look."

"No, thanks," I said. "That was my guess. Was she slim?"

The medical examiner shrugged, still bending over with a hand on the edge of the tarpaulin. He peeled it back again. I looked away. From the corner of my eye I could see him bend over and pinch some flesh on the one leg. I looked away harder.

"No," he said. "I'd say she was fleshy — not fat, mind you, but sort of, you know, buxom. Mae West, say."

"That would make her not one of the Sternwood girls," I said.

"Body hair's black," the medical examiner said.

"Carmen was blonde," I said.

Ohls nodded.

"Who found her?" he said to one of the sheriff's deputies.

"Couple high school kids had three quarts of beer," the deputy said, "slid down here in the woods to drink it and stumbled right on her. Probably take care of their underaged drinking for a while."

"Every cloud," Ohls said. "Lemme talk to them, and the officer that found the matchbook."

He climbed back up the banking to the road with me behind him. By the time I got to the road my shirt collar was limp and I could feel the sweat trickling down my spine. I leaned against the car while Ohls talked to the scared kids and to the young L.A. cop that had discovered the purse with the matchbook. Above us a little way the hill crested and Beverly Glen turned and headed down into the valley. Ventura, Sherman Oaks, people in ranch houses with two bedrooms and GI mortgages. People with kids, coming home from work, sitting down to supper, talking about the job and about the weather and about baseball and the stock market. None of them thinking anything about a one-legged half of a female body with the blood long since drained from it lying in the leaf mulch at the bottom of an arroyo off Beverly Glen. None of them were talking about that or thinking about it. But I was and I'd think about it for a long time.

Ohls came back to the car when he finished with the witnesses. He jerked his head at me and we got in and headed back toward Hollywood.

"Why don't you kind of tell me about what it is exactly that you're doing with Carmen Sternwood," he said.

I told him what I knew except for the part about Eddie Mars and Vivian. I left that out for no particular reason, except there's never any need for cops to know everything. And there was something about telling him that Vivian was with Eddie Mars that I didn't like.

"This Bonsentir," Ohls said. "He's got so much clout that he doesn't need to co-operate."

"That's what he says."

"And Al Gregory says so?"

"Yeah," I said.

"And he's up the top of Coldwater Canyon?" Ohls said.

"Yeah."

Ohls wrenched the car around and headed up Beverly Drive.

"Let's you and me go give his chain a jangle," Ohls said.

13

Ohls showed the slick-haired guy at the door his buzzer and said he was here to see Dr. Bonsentir. The slick-haired guy gave me the fisheye and said to Ohls, "May I enquire what it's about, officer?"

"Lieutenant," Ohls said, "not officer. And it's about police business which ain't your business so hustle it up."

The slick-haired man ushered us into the foyer and excused himself and walked away with his shoulders hunched in a stiff angle.

"You've hurt his feelings," I said.

"I do that," Ohls said.

We waited in front of the founder's picture for a couple of minutes and then the slick-haired guy brought his hurt feelings back into the foyer and with him came the Muscle Beach boy that I'd last seen snoozing on a chaise in the backyard.

He gave me a long stare and then said to Ohls, "What is it you want, Lieutenant?"

Ohls looked tired.

"Not you," he said to the beachboy. "I wanted you, I'd go out to Venice. I could get fifty like you in Venice."

"You think so?" the beachboy said.

"Listen, sonny, if you would like to go downtown and dance with me in the back room where the boys pitch pennies against the wall, you keep talking to me like I wasn't a cop. I want to see your boss, and it better be very damned quick."

The beachboy reddened, but he didn't say anything. He turned and went back in through the big door that led to Bonsentir's office, and in another minute he returned and beckoned us to follow.

Bonsentir was at his desk again. His tie up tight, his vest buttoned, his white coat spotless. He was on the phone. He hung up as we entered.

"I have very little time," he said. "Please make this as brief as possible."

"I'm investigating a murder," Ohls said. "Marlowe here is helping me. Not heavy-weight stuff like you do, but it keeps me from hanging around poolrooms. Carmen Sternwood is a possible witness in the murder and I want to question her."

"I'm sorry, Lieutenant . . . Ohls is it? Miss Sternwood has been discharged."

"In whose care?" I said.

"In her own, Mr. Marlowe." Bonsentir's face was beatific. He had his fingers steepled near the point of his chin.

"She's fully cured of her problems."

"How about Mrs. Swayze?" I said. "We'll talk with her, then."

"Mrs. Swayze too has been discharged," Bonsentir said. "We have great success in returning our patients to the pursuit of a normal healthy life."

"I'll bet you do," Ohls said.

"Did you turn Mrs. Swayze loose on her own?" I said.

"Certainly. She's a grown woman with no further mental problems."

"I think we might just amble around a little," Ohls said.

"Without a warrant?" Bonsentir said.

"Well, well," Ohls said.

The phone rang, Bonsentir picked it up and spoke. Then he listened a moment and looked at Ohls. He held the phone out.

"It's for you, Lieutenant," he said. His face looked benevolent.

Ohls took the phone and listened. His face didn't change expression. He didn't speak.

Then he said, "Right," and hung up the phone and handed it back to Bonsentir.

"Are you satisfied, Lieutenant?" Bonsentir said.

Ohls ignored him.

"Come on, Marlowe," Ohls said. "We're leaving."

I raised my eyebrows.

"Like that," I said.

"Like that," Ohls said. "You got a lot of weight," he said to Bonsentir. "But that doesn't mean it's over."

Bonsentir nodded over his tented fingertips.

"Race," he said to the beachboy, "show these gentlemen out."

The beachboy stepped forward and took Ohls by the arm.

"Come on," he said, "let's go."

Almost negligently Ohls chopped the edge of a right hand against the beachboy's Adam's apple. He turned sort of absentmindedly and took the beachboy's right wrist in his left hand. He put his right hand up under the beachboy's armpit, leaned in with his right shoulder and threw the beachboy into the fireplace.

"We can find the way," Ohls said and went out of the room. I smiled a friendly smile at Bonsentir. And followed Ohls out.

14

Taggert Wilde, the DA for whom I had once worked, was a plump man with clear blue eyes that managed to look at the same time friendly and expressionless. He was from an old Los Angeles family and had been DA for quite some time now. Ohls and I sat in his office while Wilde lit a thin, dappled cigar and got his feet in just the right position on the pulled-out lower drawer of his massive oak desk. On the walls around the office were muted paintings of serious-looking men in suits. Probably Wilde's predecessors in office, though they might have been his relatives.

"Doesn't mean that Bonsentir is untouchable, Bernie," Wilde said. "There are ways of handling things. But it does mean you can't go up there and roust him whenever you feel like it. None of this should surprise you."

"It doesn't surprise me," Ohls said calmly. "But I don't have to like it."

"No, you don't," Wilde said. "Hell, Bernie, I don't like it all that terribly much either.

But it's a big rough wide open country, and it's the way cities are run these days."

"Who supplies the juice?" I said.

Wilde shook his head.

"You know better, Marlowe," he said. "It's not that simple."

"What do you know about Randolph Simpson?" I said.

Wilde's face got very still. "What about Randolph Simpson?" he said.

"Mrs. Swayze, who's now supposed to have been discharged, told me that Carmen was with him," I said. "Vivian told me she knew him. I went up there and couldn't get in. Every time I mention his name the people I mention his name to get the same look you've got."

Wilde took his cigar out and looked at the tip and put it back in his mouth. He clasped both hands back of his head and looked up at the ceiling, balancing his spring swivel chair with one oxford shoe tip on the desk drawer, his other leg crossed over it. He allowed himself to teeter back and forth like that.

"Randolph Simpson is Bonsentir's clout," Wilde said finally.

"I knew that," I said. "He lives in some kind of castle up in the Santa Monica Mountains."

116

Wilde nodded slowly, still gazing up at the ceiling.

"It doesn't make any sense to say that Simpson is rich," Wilde said. "It's a meaningless phrase when you're talking about a man like Simpson. He has more wealth than many countries. He has resources that go with having that kind of money. He can literally buy anything."

"And has," I said.

"I'm an elected official, Marlowe. I try to do the job as decently as I'm permitted. But I am also part of a larger government and social entity, and as such am not an entirely free agent."

"Sure," I said.

"When you worked here you couldn't tolerate that," Wilde went on. "I understand that and I can respect it. But if the community is to function there must also be people who can tolerate working inside a system, however compromised."

"Do I salute?" I said. "Maybe stand at attention and sing 'Yankee Doodle'?"

Wilde's feet came off the desk drawer and his chair snapped forward and his eyes came level with mine.

"No," he snapped, "but you might sit still and listen and learn whatever there is to learn about Simpson. Lieutenant Ohls is bound by many of the constraints that bind me. But you are not."

I sat back in my chair and got out a cigarette and got it burning. Ohls grinned at me.

"Randolph Simpson inherited an unspeakable fortune when he was twenty-one," Wilde said. "Oil mostly, which is how he knows the Sternwoods, and some manufacturing. He tripled it in ten years and doubled that in the next five years. He plays golf regularly with the speaker of the California State Assembly. He is a close associate of both the governor of this state and the mayor of this city. His cousin is the senior senator from California, and the president of the United States comes several times a year and spends time with him at a place Simpson has in the desert. He contributes heavily and often to all of these people's election campaigns and those of a hundred aldermen and assemblymen and ward heelers of all levels that you and I may never have heard of but who turn the cranks that move things in this city."

Wilde inhaled a little smoke, savored it, let it out slowly in a thin blue stream and looked appreciatively at it as it hung in the close air of his office. Outside his window the evening was beginning to settle. Wilde continued.

"There have been a couple of marriages

that didn't work out, which he settled with money, the way he settles everything else. One of the wives filed a complaint against him alleging abusive treatment, but it never went anywhere. Whether she was bought off or scared off or Simpson simply had it squelched, I don't know. Probably all three. There was a squabble in a restaurant in Bay City a few years back when some tourist tried to take his picture and a couple of Simpson's bodyguards got rough. But nothing came of that. I have heard it said that he has peculiar sexual preferences and that some of them tend to break the rules. But no one's ever gotten near to charging him with anything, let alone getting him into court."

"What kind of sexual preferences?" I said.

Wilde took another satisfied puff on his cigar. He eased the smoke out carefully. He held the cigar out and looked at it as if to reassure himself that it was as good as it smoked. Then he said, "Sadomasochistic."

"Sounds to me like he'd suit little Carmen just fine," Ohls said.

"Fine," I said.

"He is a very dangerous man, Marlowe," Wilde said. "We can't help you unless you have evidence so unimpeachable that he can't buy it off or scare it off or cover it up or bury it."

"Or you," Ohls said.

"Stop trying to cheer me up, Bernie," I said.

"You can't go up against him alone," Wilde said. "And neither Lieutenant Ohls nor I can help you until you have incontrovertible evidence against him of whatever he may have done."

"It sounds to me like you want me to nail this guy for you," I said.

Wilde smiled without speaking. I looked at Ohls. He had shaken one of his little cigars loose from the tin in which they came and was about to light up.

"Anyone say something like that, peeper?" Ohls said. "I didn't hear anything like that said. What you got from us is permission to go ahead and look for the girl, like you was hired to do."

"I don't need your permission," I said.

"So, good," Ohls said. "So whyn't you get the hell out of here and start looking?"

I stood up.

"You guys are a scream," I said. "Thanks for nothing at all."

"Go carefully, Marlowe," Wilde said.

"Sure thing," I said.

Ohls grinned humorlessly at me past his toy cigar.

"Call anytime, peeper," he said.

I turned and left Wilde's office and went downstairs and caught a cab home.

15

I was living that year in the Hobart Arms on Franklin just west of Kenmore. It was where I went after I picked up my car. I had found and then lost a dippy old lady trying to see her house, and parts of another lady. And Taggert Wilde and Ohls and Bonsentir — I'd found all of them. I'd even found Randolph Simpson, for all the good it did me. Unfortunately I wasn't supposed to find them. I was supposed to find Carmen Sternwood, and I was setting a record for not finding her.

The apartment had the closed-up smell that empty places get, the smell of nobody home. It was a smell I knew well, though I'd never gotten used to it. I went and opened the windows and let the hot air move vaguely around. It didn't do much to the atmosphere inside. It hadn't been doing a hell of a lot for the atmosphere outside. I got a bottle of Vat 69 out of the kitchen cabinet, and built myself a tall scotch and water, took it into the living room, and looked down onto Franklin Avenue. There were the usual cars parked along the sidewalk, I'd stared down at them a lot in the late afternoon with a drink in my hand and no one else around. The street was far enough below so that not much noise drifted up, mostly I heard the silence behind me in the room, almost tangible, shimmering in the late summer afternoon like the heat waves that miraged up from the surface of the avenue. After you're alone long enough you get used to it. Almost.

Parked across the street halfway down the block toward Alexandria was a car that didn't fit into the pattern my eyes automatically expected. It was bigger and newer than most cars that park in my neighborhood, and its motor was idling. I looked at it harder, but the sun glancing off the windows made it impossible to see inside. I watched it for a while and sipped my drink. When the drink was gone I went back in and bought myself another one and looked at the chess puzzle set up on the table. It didn't interest me. Kings and Queens and Knights seemed irrelevant. I did feel some kinship with the pawns. I sipped a little more of my drink and went and looked out the window again. The Buick was still there. That was okay. I was still here.

There had to be a reason a mutilated corpse showed up with the Sternwoods' phone number in her purse. Everyone was assuming it was Carmen's number but it was also Vivian's. Hell, it was also Norris's number and the horsefaced maid's. Still, Carmen was a good bet. It was at least one angle, and it would make sense if Carmen and the unnamed cut-up lady had crossed paths at the Resthaven Sanitarium, or maybe they were both palsy with Randolph Simpson, or maybe they met at the May Company, trying on aprons, and took an instant liking to each other.

My drink was gone. I went to the kitchen and rinsed out the glass and put it away. I looked at my chess puzzle again, shook my head, went back to the window and stared down for a while at the black Buick. And the phone rang.

The voice I heard belonged to Vincent Norris.

"Mr. Marlowe, Mrs. Regan would like very much to see you this evening, if you could stop by at your first convenience."

"Cops been there?" I said.

"I dare say they have, sir. And Mrs. Regan seems visibly upset by their visit. I do urge you to come and visit, sir."

"You're my employer, Norris. You urge, I comply."

"Quite so, sir. Thank you, sir."

"Tell Mrs. Regan I'll be there as soon as

I break my date with the Countess of Columbia," I said.

"I hope the Countess will understand, sir."

"Yeah," I said. "I'm sure she will."

I hung up and got a gun out of the desk drawer and slipped on a shoulder holster. Then I went down and got in my car and headed west on Franklin past the Buick. By the time I reached Normandie the Buick was behind me, and it stayed behind me all the way to Alta Brea Crescent.

It was a competent tail job by a guy who didn't seem to care if I made him. He stayed up close, no more than two cars away, and didn't try to get any closer. It appeared that he just wanted to know where I was going. After Alta Brea Crescent, I didn't know either.

16

Vivian Sternwood's room was still too white and too high and too big. And the drapes still spilled onto the floor as if the interior decorator had measured wrong. She was in white silk pajamas this evening and was drinking scotch. She might have drunk quite a lot of it from the hard bright look in her eyes. But her speech was clear. When I came in she was sprawled on some kind of white satin fainting couch, one white satin slipper hung from her foot, the other was on the floor.

"Well, Marlowe," she said when the maid had shut the door behind me, "the bargain basement Lancelot. How's the maiden rescuing going?"

I let that ride, there was nothing in it for me.

"Have a drink," Vivian said. She made a fluttering hand gesture at a silver ice bucket and a bottle of scotch and some glasses and tongs. I mixed up a light one and squirted some seltzer in from the silver filigreed siphon. I made a slight here's-to-you gesture with the glass and took a swallow. It was better scotch than I was used to.

"Tired of drinking alone?" I said.

"Tired of not getting drunk," she said. "I've been trying for the last couple of hours."

"Boys with the steel-toed shoes been tramping around on your rug?" I said.

She nodded and took a long drink. I could tell from the color that it was mostly scotch and very little soda. She nodded slowly.

"My God, Marlowe, that woman . . ."

"Yeah."

"You saw her?"

"Yeah."

"Carmen . . ." she said and let it trail off. She took a cigarette from a lacquer box beside her and put it in her mouth and leaned slightly toward me. I got up and put a match to it for her and shook the match out and dropped it in the silver ashtray beside the lacquer box.

"What about Carmen?" I said.

"The woman had her phone number."

"Or yours," I said.

"Marlowe, people do not walk around with my phone number written on the inside of matchbooks. It had to be Carmen."

"Any ideas?" I said.

Vivian shook her head and drank again and took a deep lungful of smoke and let it drift out slowly. We were quiet. Vivian drank the rest of her drink and held the empty glass out toward me. I got up and took it and mixed her a fresh one.

"Lots of scotch, please," she said. "I need to get drunk awfully damned badly."

I gave her the new drink and waited, nursing mine.

"You don't think . . ." She stopped and looked into her glass for a moment before she drank. Then she tried again.

"You don't think Carmen . . . could have . . ."

"Could have killed the woman?"

"Or helped someone."

The room ached with silence as the question hung there between us.

"You know her better than anyone," I said. "Could she do that?"

Vivian shrugged. The skin was very tight on her face, and the lines at the corners of her mouth were harshly etched into her pale skin. I thought about Carmen, about the time I'd come home and found her naked in my bed and I'd turned her down.

Her teeth parted and a faint hissing noise came out of her mouth. She didn't answer me. I went out to the kitchenette and got out some scotch and fizzwater and mixed a couple of highballs. I didn't have anything really exciting to drink, like nitroglycerine or distilled tiger's breath. She hadn't moved when I got back with the glasses. The hissing had stopped. Her eyes were dead again. Her lips started to smile at me. Then she sat up suddenly and threw all the covers off her body and reached.

"Gimme."

"When you're dressed. Not until *you're dressed."*

I put the two glasses down on the card table and sat down myself and lit another cigarette. "Go ahead. I won't watch you."

I looked away. Then I was aware of the hissing noise very sudden and sharp. It startled me into looking at her again. She sat there naked, propped on her hands, her mouth open a little, her face like scraped bone. The hissing noise came tearing out of her mouth as if she had nothing to do with it. There was something behind her eyes, blank as they were, that I had never seen in a woman's eyes. . . .

She had left finally, but she didn't forget that I'd rejected her.

"You've seen her," Vivian said. "She's not right. Maybe, if she were drinking exotic things and mixing them, and thought it would

129

be giggly fun . . ."

Vivian let the sentence hang.

"Yes," I said.

"And the next day remember nothing," Vivian said.

We were quiet.

"I don't know," I said. "Probably too hard a job, the simple physical labor of dismemberment, for a small girl to do alone. She might have been an accessory, though. No way to know."

"You have to find her, Marlowe."

"Yeah? Maybe if somebody would tell me something, I might just do that."

"Tell you what?"

"Where she might be. How she got to Bonsentir. What the connection is with Randolph Simpson. Why you wanted me out of the thing and told me Eddie Mars was taking care of everything. What the hell you're doing with Eddie Mars anyway. Things like that."

She held my gaze angrily for a minute and then her face began to crumble. She started to cry. With the tears running down her face she said, "Hold me, damn you, Marlowe. Put your arms around me."

I moved over onto the couch and put my arms around her. She arched up into my arms and buried her face against my chest and sobbed. Her body shook with every sob as if the sound was forced out of her against her will. After maybe five minutes that seemed no longer than the Thirty Years War she began to calm down. The sobs spaced out more and finally stopped. She lay still in my arms, her face against my chest, her arms locked around my neck, her body pressed against me hard. Finally she lifted her face and kissed me. There was no contrivance this time. I kissed her back. She opened her mouth.

Without taking her lips from mine she murmured "yes, yes."

I didn't hear anyone say "no."

When it was over, we lay still, half dressed and breathless together on her couch, which was a little narrow for two people, one of whom weighed 190.

"I wonder sometimes," Vivian said, "why it had to be me. Why I have to take care of this childish pervert."

"I guess because there isn't anyone else," I said.

Vivian lay with her head in the crook of my arm.

"She was always . . . twisted. When we were little girls in polka-dot dresses, she was always, somehow, corrupt, as if she were born with something nasty infesting her soul."

"Ever try to get her cured?" I said.

Vivian's head stirred on my arm. She held the fingers of that arm in her right hand and pressed them occasionally against her cheek as she talked.

"I've taken her to Europe, sanitariums, private hospitals, the best analysts. She remains a depraved child. Maybe it's my mother's blood, or the mix of it with the Sternwoods'. My mother died when we were very young. My father would never speak of her."

"So you finally gave up on Carmen and tried to find somewhere to keep her out of trouble."

"I need a life, Marlowe. I need a chance to love someone, to get free of her."

"So you shipped her off to Dr. Bonsentir, and his needles, and his pills, and his security."

"Yes," Vivian said. "I'm not ashamed of that. Resthaven is well regarded, and Dr. Bonsentir is a specialist in sexually related personality disorders."

"I'll bet he is," I said. "How'd you find him?"

She said something I couldn't hear.

"I didn't get that," I said.

"Randolph Simpson," she said in a voice that came out too loud because she was forcing it.

"Ah yes," I said. "The old family friend."

"My father knew him. When my father was younger he did some business with his family."

"The first time I asked, you said you didn't know him."

"He requires anonymity," Vivian said.

"I'll bet he does," I said.

"In truth he frightens me. He told me to tell no one he'd helped me with Carmen, and when you asked I was afraid."

"You think Carmen's with him?"

"I don't know." I could hear her breath go in shakily and come out the same way. "I guess I don't want to know."

"So where's Mars come in?"

"I asked Eddie to see if he could find out where Carmen was."

"And he agreed?"

"Yes. He helped me with Carmen before. He knows about her."

"What's he get out of it?"

"Nothing. It's just a favor to me."

"Guys like Mars don't do favors," I said. "He gets something."

"Maybe you wouldn't understand," Vivian said. "But Eddie Mars loves me."

"I might understand that, but I'm not sure I understand it in a gee like Eddie."

"I know. I know what Eddie is, but he is capable of love, Marlowe, and he loves me."

"How about you?" I said.

"Do I love him?"

"Un huh."

"No, I don't suppose I do. But it would be easy to. Eddie's a powerful man. He has money. He has influence. He's tough and things don't scare him."

"And he's crooked as a con man's smile," I said.

"Maybe, but if you've been alone and a woman and frightened, power and influence and money and tough looks like it might be enough."

"What about me?" I said.

She paused, rubbing the back of my hand against her cheek.

"You're different, Marlowe."

I had nothing to add to that. I took a cigarette from her lacquered box and lit it and passed it to her and took another and lit it for myself. We lay quietly smoking.

"You think she's with Simpson?" I said.

She took in some smoke. When she let it out it drifted up and hung wispily above us as we lay on our backs.

"I don't know," she said. "I'm afraid that she could be."

"Tell me about him," I said.

Again the slow inhale and the smoke drifting lazily up.

"He's the . . . oddest man I know. He plays golf, for instance, on his own golf course, just him and his partner, and the bodyguards."

"The boys in the dark suits," I said. "I've met several of them."

"They surround him wherever he goes."

"Swell," I said.

"He's been married, but he's not married now, and he likes girls, but never for very long. And they always have to be brought to his home. And, ah, they, ah, all have to have a medical examination."

"See how easy I am," I said.

"Um."

"You think Simpson got you to send Carmen to Bonsentir so Bonsentir could hand her along?"

"I don't know," Vivian said. "I'm afraid to know. I kept hoping maybe Eddie would somehow take care of it."

"He's tight with Bonsentir?"

"Simpson? Yes. He's more than that — he's, ah, he's dependent on him, I think."

"Dependent?"

"He's his doctor, but more than that he seems to be like a confessor, some sort of priest, as well as physician."

"And Eddie wouldn't talk to me about any of this when I asked him because you'd told him it was hush-hush."

"Yes. If Randolph's confidence is violated he is very unpredictable. It's not even that he's cruel, though he probably is. It's that he is so rich, so indescribably wealthy, that he does whatever he will, without thought, simply because he can."

"I'm glad for him," I said. "I'll settle for just ordinary riches, like yours. Shall we fly off to Tahiti and build a fairy-tale castle?"

"I wish we could," Vivian said. "It would be very attractive to think about it."

"You don't know who might be tailing me in a black Buick sedan, do you?"

Her whole body stiffened.

"My God," she said. "What if it's Randolph?"

"I'll take care of Randolph," I said. "He'll think he was in an avalanche."

"Maybe it's not Randolph," she said.

"Maybe not," I said. "Maybe it's Eddie. Or maybe it's the cops, though they don't usually do tail jobs in Buicks. Or maybe kindly Dr. Claude is having me followed. Or maybe it's a member of the Philip Marlowe Fan Club trying to get up her courage to ask for my autograph."

"Will you take care of me, Marlowe?"

"Sure thing," I said. "And I'll find Carmen too. I was tired of chess puzzles anyway."

17

The Cypress Club was hopping. A doorman that was dressed like an admiral in the Yugoslavian navy opened the doors for me and I went into the hushed tension of the gambling club. I shook my head at the hat check girl and kept my hat on my head. In the main room there were people gathered under lowered lights around the tables. Everyone looked as if they were watching surgery. No one talked loudly, the bored voices of the dealers droned their dealer patter, the sound of chips and the whir of the roulette wheel was as loud as any human voice. It was never clear to me why people gambled since they seemed to enjoy it so little.

I drifted into the bar and ordered a Bacardi cocktail.

"Eddie around?" I said to the bartender.

"Don't know no Eddie, pal."

"Sure you don't," I said. "You never heard of Eddie Mars. He doesn't own this clip joint. You don't know who owns it. You just work here."

"If it turned out that I did know this

Eddie guy, who should I say was asking?"

"Marlowe," I said.

The bartender polished the bartop vigorously.

"I see anybody might know this Eddie, I'll make mention of your name."

"That'd be dandy," I said.

The bartender moved on down the bar. I turned and looked out at the main room. A tall jasper with a pencil moustache was making thousand-dollar bets at the baccarat table and losing them. He was obviously drunk and his face was very flushed. A silver-blonde lady with a mink stole and a long cigarette holder was tugging at his arm and crying. He paid her no mind. Just kept laying down the big pictures and losing them and taking another one out of the slim ostrich-skin wallet he took from his inside pocket. Finally the blonde swore at him and released his arm and stalked out of the place. The tall thin guy never looked at her, or after her when she left.

The bartender moved back down the bar toward me.

"Be easier if he just mailed Mars a check," I said, nodding at the tall drunk losing his money.

"Ain't that the truth," the bartender said. He nodded past my shoulder. "Mr. Mars will see you now," he said.

I turned and Eddie Mars was there, a different gray suit and shirt. This time with a sapphire tie pin in a different gray tie.

"Heard you were asking about me, soldier."

"Yeah. We need to talk."

Mars nodded and slid onto the barstool next to me. He waited.

"I talked with Vivian tonight," I said.

Mars' face showed nothing.

"She told me what she knows about Carmen and Bonsentir and Simpson and how you said you'd help her because you love her."

"She told you a lot, soldier."

"Yeah. She's in trouble and she knows it," I said. "She's looking for help."

"So why you telling me this?" Mars said. He took a cigarette out of a silver case and put it in his mouth. The bartender appeared and lit it and moved away.

"I figure we're both working the same side of the street this time. I want to know what you know."

Mars smiled.

"You and me, huh soldier? What a pair."

"I don't like it, Eddie. And I don't like you. But if you got anything I can use, I'll take it."

"Fair enough, soldier. Nice to know where we stand."

"What do you know?" I said.

"What do I get from telling you?"

"I tell people you're nice," I said.

"Yeah?"

"And I won't be stepping all over you and your boys while I'm looking for Carmen."

"Stepping on anything of mine will get you a slow ride in a pine box, soldier."

"One of the things I don't like about you, Eddie," I said. "Inside the hand-tailored suits and the fancy manners you're a goon, just like you were when you started."

"Calling each other names isn't going to get this deal done, soldier. And it could get you a bad case of bruises."

"I've had bruises before," I said. "I love bruises. Bruises are my friends. What do you know about Carmen? Remind yourself you're doing this for Vivian."

"You don't believe it, do you, Marlowe? That a guy like me could go soft for a dame like Vivian Sternwood."

"I believe you could go soft, Eddie. I don't believe you could go generous. An angle will turn up in here somewhere. Like it did before."

Mars shook his head.

"You're hard to like, Marlowe. I'll say that for you."

I waited.

"Carmen's with Simpson all right. He took her from the sanitarium. Bonsentir's a high-priced pimp. He runs this clinic for people with sex problems, and then he rents out the juicy ones to a list of very high-priced clients."

"Like Simpson," I said.

"Like Simpson," Mars said.

"He's the one sent her there in the first place," I said.

Mars shook his head again and took a long drag on his cigarette.

"Christ," Mars said, "it's not like Carmen was hard. Why go through all that rigmarole of sending her through his pimp?"

"So she'd be medically certified," I said.

Mars looked startled.

"Medically?"

"Disease free," I said. "Simpson's phobic about venereal diseases."

"Creep," Mars said.

"So he gets her committed to a sanitarium where she'll be examined and found healthy and passed on to him."

"How you know so much about Simpson?"

"Vivian told me," I said.

"Funny she didn't tell me."

"I don't think Vivian tells anybody everything," I said. "I think she's learned not to be too trusting."

"She can trust me," Mars said.

"Sure she can, Eddie. I can too, everybody can."

Mars wasn't listening to me. He was thinking about other things. Things I wouldn't ever get to hear. Maybe he did love her. Maybe I did too.

"I don't know much about Simpson. But I know you can't take him."

"I'll take him," I said.

Mars stubbed his cigarette out in the ashtray on the bar.

"Sure you will, soldier. You keep thinking that."

"You know where Simpson's got her?" I said.

He shook his head.

"Simpson's got places everywhere," Mars said. "You never know which place he's at and no one ever says. He's got three dozen limousines and a fleet of private planes and God knows what all. We're looking into it, but we're not too close yet."

The man at the baccarat table was out of thousands. He said something loud and nasty to the dealer. Mars didn't turn his head but his eyes shifted over there.

"You got anything else to add that would help me?" I said.

"No," Mars said. His eyes stayed on the

tall geek with the moustache. "I'm not sure anything will help you, soldier."

The tall geek said something even nastier. Mars nodded slightly and the pasty-faced blond gunsel that I'd met before appeared out of the shadows and stood next to the tall drunk. He murmured something into the drunk's ear and the drunk turned and tried to shove him away. The blond guy made a movement and the tall drunk doubled up suddenly with a look of shock on his face. The blond guy straightened him up gently with one hand on each shoulder and turned him slowly toward the door. He draped one arm over the drunk's shoulder and began to walk him toward the door. As they passed I got a look at the drunk's face. He looked sick.

"Hard running a dignified place," Mars said sadly.

"Ain't it the truth," I said. "You let me know if anything shows?"

Mars turned and looked at me with no visible feeling.

"Like you said, soldier, we aren't friends. You do your peekaboo work. I'll try to run a nice club. And we won't get in each other's way. Okay?"

"Ain't love grand," I said and got up and got out of there.

18

When I got to the Hobart Arms, I noticed the black Buick was parked across the street. The motor was off this time, and it seemed to be empty. I parked a couple of spaces past it and walked back toward my building along Franklin. As I went up the steps a figure detached from the shadow of the shrubs and pointed a gun at me. Another figure appeared behind me.

"Hold it right there, pally," a voice said. It was a flat voice with very little in it that was human. A flashlight beam hit me in the eyes.

I held it right there. Behind me I felt the press of a gun barrel against my spine, in the small of my back. I could hear its owner's breath in my ear. Feel it on my neck. There was no one on the street, nobody in sight.

"Got a message for you, pally," the flat voice said. He was out of sight behind the brightness of the flashlight.

"Who's your voice coach?" I said. "You sound like a bad movie."

"Don't look for Carmen Sternwood anymore," the flat voice said. "Don't pay any attention to Randolph Simpson. Don't go near Dr. Bonsentir."

"Okay if I eat a pitted prune now and then?" I said.

The voice went on as if it were a recording.

"This is the only warning you'll get. You don't behave and the next one will be fatal."

"Anything else?" I said.

"Yeah," the voice said, "one other thing."

From behind the blinding light a fist appeared. I caught the glint of brass knuckles for a moment before they exploded against my jaw. I staggered back against the gunman behind me. Bright lights exploded in front of my eyes. I kicked the flat voice in the general area of the stomach and heard him gasp and then something erupted against the side of my head and the lights coalesced into a brilliant starburst and then blackness into which I slid as peacefully as a drunken seal.

I was drifting through a black sea and above me in the light I could see Carmen and Vivian dancing with a man I didn't know while Claude Bonsentir played the violin. I tried to swim upward toward them but the sea was thick and cold and I wasn't making any progress.

When I woke up it was raining. I was on

my back with an iron ache in my head and the rain coming down steadily in my face, bright as it passed through the light from the double glass doors to my building. The pain in my head rang like an anvil when I moved. I closed my eyes and lay perfectly still. *Okay, Marlowe, you're a tough guy. You can get up. Just roll over on your side.* I tried it and felt my stomach heave. I held still until it passed. *Attaboy, Marlowe, halfway there. Now get your eyes open. Good boy. Now get to one knee. Nothing to it, you've been sapped before.* I stayed there balanced on one knee while the rainy night swirled around me and slowly came to a halt. I got my feet under me and stood. The world moved in a circle again and I swayed with it until it settled back down. *Easy.*

There was a soft angry swelling behind my ear, and a gash on my jawline that felt as if it had bled and scabbed over. I felt my pockets. Nothing was missing. The gun was still under my arm where it had stayed dry while I was getting socked and sapped. Good thing I hadn't gotten it out. It would be all wet now.

I got the key in the lock after a couple of tries and opened the doors and went in. Upstairs I looked at myself in the mirror. I looked like I had been dragged in by a cat and rejected. I got some ice from the refrigerator and put it in a facecloth and held it against the bruise on the back of my head. When I took the facecloth away there was a little blood on it. All my teeth seemed to be in the right place and still anchored.

I sat in a chair near the window and looked out at the rain and let the ice rest against the back of my head. There was no sign on the street below of the black Buick.

The fact that someone, probably Simpson, didn't want me looking into this case wasn't a news flash. I knew that before. Now I knew how much they didn't want me.

Finally I reached the phone over and called Bernie Ohls at home.

"You know what time it is?" he said when he answered.

"I need the owner of a black Buick sedan, late model, California tags." I gave him the number.

"Sure, Marlowe. I was reading my kid a story, but hell, I'll go right down and open up the hall of records and look this up personal and hand-carry it right over to you."

"Couple of guys driving that thing roughed me up, told me to stay away from the Carmen Sternwood case."

"Gee, I hope it didn't spoil your good looks, Marlowe."

147

"I figure it's Simpson, but maybe the license plates will tell me something."

"And maybe they won't," Ohls said. "I'll call you in the morning."

"You got an ID yet on the corpse off Beverly Glen?"

"Tentative," Ohls said. "Neighborhood dog showed up with the hand. Proud as hell, wagging his tail. His owner nearly croaked. Assuming it goes with the other parts of the body, the victim is a B-picture actress named Lola Monforte. Last known address was a flop on Melrose, but she hasn't been there in several months."

"That's it?"

"That's all so far," Ohls said. "Us coppers just have to plod along, you know. We ain't geniuses like you private-license boys. I figure you'll have it all solved for us by the time I get you this car registration."

"Any connection to Bonsentir? Or Simpson?"

"Don't know," Ohls said. "Hard to find out."

Ohls hung up. Outside the rain came down in a light steady drizzle. Not hard enough to wash gullies in the canyons where people built expensive houses on sand and runoff. Just enough to keep the reservoirs from drying up and to help the lawns a little. I opened the window. The damp mysterious smell of a wet night came in.

The ache in my head had dulled. My collar was soaked from the ice pack and I dropped the nearly melted cubes on the rug. It was after ten on a rainy night in the city of the angels. No one knocked on the door. No one called. No one was interested in my travel plans. No one seemed much concerned about my health.

I called Vivian Regan. The phone rang a long time before the horsefaced maid answered. She was sorry but Mrs. Regan had taken a sleeping pill and gone to bed. Was there a message? No message. I hung up the phone and went back to staring at the misting rain which drifted down as silently as snow.

19

Ohls called while I was drinking my second cup of coffee and trying to decide about breakfast. My head felt like the inside of a snare drum.

"Buick's registered to an outfit called Neville Realty Trust, got an address in the Neville Valley, up north."

I got a pencil. Ohls gave me the address.

"Any names attached?" I said.

"Not on the registration. I haven't looked any further. Figure that's your job."

"Sure," I said. "No one sapped you."

"My heart bleeds," Ohls said and hung up.

In my office with coffee and a roll I'd picked up in the drugstore downstairs, I got out my map book. The Neville Valley was maybe 200 miles northeast of Los Angeles on the other side of the San Gabriel Mountains.

I called my client.

When Norris came on the phone, I said, "Marlowe. With a report."

"How very kind of you, Mr. Marlowe," Norris said.

"Looking for Carmen so far has got me

threatened by a tough Mexican, involved in a mutilation murder, slugged with brass knuckles and sapped by person or persons unknown."

"Good heavens, sir, I never wanted you to get hurt."

"Nor did I, Norris," I said, "but the point is this thing is a much larger thing than it looked like it was going to be."

"As I have said, sir, the General left me well provided for. I could pay you a rather handsome fee."

"No need for that, Norris. There's so much money floating around the fringes of this case that it's hard not to twist an ankle stepping over it. I'll find a fee okay. But it seems like more dangerous going than either of us thought when I started."

"I anticipated only whatever danger Miss Carmen presented, sir."

"Which is not inconsiderable. But it's beginning to look attractive to me now."

"Do you wish to withdraw, sir?"

"You bet I do," I said. "But I won't. I just wanted you to know what was happening."

"I rather expected that you would not withdraw, sir. Might you give me some of the details?"

I did.

When I was through there was a quiet

pause. Then Norris said, "I'm sure you will be adequate to the task, Mr. Marlowe."

"I'm sure I will too, Norris," I said. "I would be even more adequate if I knew exactly what the task was."

"From my perspective, sir, if I may, it is to find Miss Carmen, sir."

"Yes, Norris, I guess it is."

We hung up. I put my map book under my arm, made sure I had my gun and some extra cartridges. It hadn't done me any good yet, but it made me feel like a detective. Then I locked the office and went out to my car.

It took about five hours to drive up to Neville Valley. I got there a little after two in the afternoon, with a high hard sky glaring down and the temperature in the nineties.

Neville Valley was the name of a region, and a town in the center of the region. The region was a drab lowland in the foothills with the Neville River running through the center of it. Right beside the river the valley was lush, but a mile from the river was near desert land, parched, infertile, and hard-scrabble. The town of Neville Valley was at the point where the river cascaded over a small decline strewn with boulders and provided the only white water probably in a thousand square miles. It was the only place where the river ran fast, before it slowed into a series of huge looping meanders that made a convoluted green stripe down the center of the broad ugly valley.

I pulled my car, nose in, on the parking apron in front of a low white building with a broad front porch that ran the length of it. A sign on the roof of the porch said THE RIVER RUN INN. There was a double screen door leading into a dark lobby with a dark oak desk along the left wall and a broad staircase directly opposite the entrance. To the right was a combination dining room and bar, which seemed empty. Behind the desk was a pretty, red-haired girl in a white peasant blouse. The red hair was held in check by a white scarf tied behind her neck. She had white skin and a scatter of freckles across the cheekbones and when she smiled dimples appeared in each cheek.

"You look like a man who's driven a long way," she said when I came to register.

"Bar open?" I said.

"Will be as soon as you get registered and the bartender gets in there."

"Where is he now?" I said.

Her cheeks dimpled. "Registering you," she said.

I grinned at her.

"Okay then," I said. "I'll hurry."

When I got through signing in and she'd given me a room key and asked about luggage and been informed that I was wearing it, we retired to the bar. I sat on a stool, she opened the hinged bar section that allowed her in behind it and came down the bar top where I sat.

"What'll it be, buddy?" she said, lowering her voice and sounding as gruff as a twenty-three-year-old redhead with blue-green eyes could sound.

I ordered a gimlet. She mixed it up expertly and poured it perfectly into the glass in exactly the right amount, leaving nothing but ice in the shaker. It was cool and dark in the bar. And quiet, as only a good bar in the middle of the afternoon can be. I sipped the gimlet and let the cool bite of it run down my throat.

"Can you tell me where the Neville Realty Trust is located?" I said.

"Sure. Got a little office on Otis Street, out the hotel, turn left one block, turn right. You'll see it. Got the name right in the window."

She smiled at me again, her cheeks dimpling. Her red hair was the dark thick kind, she probably called it auburn, and it fell in soft curls to her shoulders, where the white scarf held it back from her face.

"What do they do their business in?" I asked. "Farmland? Doesn't seem much salable real estate around here."

"Not now." The redhead smiled as widely as it seemed possible to smile. "But pretty soon there will be. There's a big government project coming to the valley. Going to do a big land-reclamation with the Neville River and irrigate the whole valley. Everyone says it will mean a whole new boom for the area: farmland, tourism, growth. Everybody's excited about it. We got somebody from Washington in here every week, and a bunch of people from Sacramento. You involved in that?"

"No," I said. "I don't own much property. So the Neville Realty people are buying up farmland in anticipation of the boom?"

"Farmland?" The redhead looked startled. "No. They're buying water rights. People are getting good money for the water rights around here. Government has to acquire them to do the project, you know?"

"Sure," I said. "And Neville Realty is buying them up for the government?"

"Well, yes. I mean sure, I guess so. Everybody's real excited about it. You aren't with the government, are you?"

I shook my head.

"I didn't think so," she said. "You don't

look like somebody with the government, that's for sure. I bet you're one of those Los Angeles people interested in this. Lots of them stay here."

"That so?" I said. "What's Los Angeles got to do with this?"

"Oh, you know, money people. They're always around when anything big is happening, don't you know?"

"I do know, in fact," I said. "You make a hell of a gimlet."

"My dad used to drink them," she said. "He built this place."

"Did a good job too," I said. "Know any of the people work at Neville Realty?"

She shook her head. "Not really," she said. "They're not Neville Valley people. They came in a year or so ago and opened the office. It used to be a feed store in there before. But business was so bad that they had to sell out. Everybody's hoping this land-reclamation water project will change everything."

"What's your name?" I said.

"Wendy," she said. "Wendy Clausen."

I put out my hand.

"It's nice to meet you, Wendy," I said. She shook my hand and smiled her wide smile.

"A pleasure, Mr. Marlowe."

I thanked her for the drink and the talk

and got up and went out to visit the Neville Realty Trust. The heat, when I came out of the dim hotel lobby, was something to wade through, unyielding, implacable, and inhumane. There was almost no one on the drowsy main street as I turned left, walked a block and turned right. The only life I saw was a black and tan collie with a white chest sleeping on the front steps of a hardware store.

There was a little gravel parking lot next to the office of Neville Realty Trust. There was a Ford pickup truck parked there and a gray Mercury sedan. No black Buick. There was a big storefront-style window across the front with a black and gold sign in ornate Gothic lettering. There was a little bell on the glass-paneled front door, and when I walked in, the bell tinkled pleasantly. There were two people in the room: a fat woman with a very red face whose flowered blouse stuck to her in the heat, and a sharp-featured guy with a long chin and slick black hair. He looked happy in the heat, like one of those reptiles who need it to loosen up and come awake. A big floor fan was wasting its time in the corner of the room.

I stopped in front of the fat woman's desk. She wiped her face with a lace-embroidered handkerchief and looked up at me from the ledger that was open on her desk.

"Help you?" she said in a voice that didn't mean it.

"Like to buy some land," I said.

She shook her head, heavily, and wiped her face again. The handkerchief looked wetter than her blouse.

"Got none for sale right now," she said. "Sorry."

"How about some water rights?" I wasn't exactly sure what a water right was, but it seemed like the thing to ask.

"We got no water rights," she said. The sharpster at the other desk was concentrating on something that looked like a plot plan on his desk. He was concentrating all right, except his ears were out maybe a foot toward our conversation.

I looked surprised. "Really?" I said. "I heard you had been acquiring water rights all over the valley."

"We got none for sale," she said. The effort of talking to me seemed to be making her hotter.

"I see," I said. "Well is the, ah, owner of the firm available?"

The sharpster at the other desk leaned back in his chair and swiveled halfway around to look at me.

"We got nothing to sell, bub. Maybe you didn't quite get that."

"How surprising," I said. I was trying to sound like the kind of tycoon who would sweep in and buy up thirty trillion dollars' worth of almost anything.

"Yeah," the sharpster said, "ain't it? Now, why don't you kinda drift."

I looked puzzled. "Drift?"

"Yeah. You know — take a hike, breeze, it's a hot day and we got things to do."

"Well," I said. "I must say, I wonder how you stay in business."

I turned on my heel and stomped out. Across the street was a barbershop and next to it a drugstore. Through the front window of the drugstore I could see the corner of a soda fountain. I went across and into the drugstore. It had a marble counter and a big fountain with spigots, and spouts for syrup, in a glistening row behind it. A ceiling fan moved slowly and with little effect above me. The pharmacist was behind the fountain with his arms folded, gazing silently out at the street. He was short and slight with a bald head across which he'd plastered two or three wisps of hair. I ordered a lime rickey. He made it in a tall fluted glass and put it in front of me on top of a little paper doily. He shoved a round container of straws toward me and went back to leaning against the back counter and staring out the window.

From where I sat I could look straight out at the Neville Realty Trust.

I nodded at the office across the street. "New business in town?"

The pharmacist nodded.

"Successful?" I said.

The pharmacist nodded again.

"I understand they're buying water rights up around here."

The pharmacist became talkative. "Yep," he said.

"You done any business with them?"

"Nope."

"Know who owns the company?"

"Nope."

"Don't talk much, do you?" I said.

"Nope. Don't need to. City fella like you comes in, does all the talking anyway."

"See a lot of city people up here, do you?" I said.

"Since the government project."

"From Los Angeles?"

"Guess so."

Across the street a black Buick sedan swung into the parking lot of the Neville Realty Trust. It had the right license tags. Two men got out of the front, and the one on the passenger's side held open the rear door for a third man. All I could see of him was that he wore a seersucker suit and would be a perfect mate for the fat woman in the office. He had trouble getting out of the car, and when he did finally manage it, he paused to wipe his face with a big white handkerchief before he waddled into the office.

"Who's the fat guy?" I said.

"Don't know," the pharmacist said. "You want some more lime rickey?"

I said no, and he swooped the glass away and washed it in the little sink back there, and put it upside down on the shelf behind him. He and I sat in silence for a while.

Nothing moved across the street. Finally I got up and paid for my lime rickey.

"I'm going where I can get a little peace and quiet," I said. And went out and walked back to the River Run Inn.

20

It cooled off after midnight and I got to sleep. Showered, shaved and breakfasted, I was in my car heading back to L.A. by nine A.M. Except for the green strip along the Neville River, the land was brown and still under heat that made the landscape shimmer.

Back in my office I called Ohls and gave him the license numbers for the pickup, and the gray Mercury I had seen parked in the Neville Valley Realty Trust parking lot. Then I went downstairs to the coffee shop and had a ham sandwich and some coffee and came back upstairs and sat and dangled my feet until Ohls called back. The truck was registered to Neville Valley Realty Trust. The gray Mercury belonged to the Rancho Springs Development Corporation in Rancho Springs, California.

"You need anything else, Hawkshaw?" Ohls said.

"You show me how this all ties into Carmen Sternwood," I said.

"Be good for you," Ohls said, "to work it out yourself."

I went straight downtown to the hall of records and spent maybe an hour and a half looking up the incorporation papers that the California secretary of state's office requires of all new companies. Neville Valley Trust was in there, and the Rancho Springs Development Corp. Everything was written in the conventional language of lawyers, which is why it took me an hour and a half. But when I was through I knew that the Neville Valley Realty Trust and Rancho Springs Development Corporation were legal corporations in the State of California. And I knew that a member of the incorporating board of Rancho Springs was Claude Bonsentir.

Then I went to the library and spent another couple of hours in the periodical room reading up on the Neville Valley Land Reclamation Project. It was almost as boring as the documents of incorporation, but basically I learned that it was a part of a federal effort to reclaim barren land in the West and Southwest. The plan in Neville Valley was to use the spill from the Neville River to irrigate land all over the valley and turn it into rich farming country. There was no mention of the Neville Valley Trust in anything I read.

Driving back to Hollywood, I thought about all of this. Was Neville Valley Realty buying up water rights as representatives of the government? Were they buying the rights so they could resell them to the government at extortion-level prices? What was kindly old doctor Heal-all doing on the board of the Rancho Springs Development Corp.? And why did some employees of the Neville Valley Realty Trust come to Hollywood and pour it on me?

Back in my office I put in a call to the Bureau of Land Management's Los Angeles office. It took about a half an hour, and most of that on hold, to get anyone who even knew about the Neville Valley project, and he didn't know anything about the Neville Realty Trust. Which didn't prove that they weren't working for the government. It only proved what I already knew about the government.

I sat at my desk with the window open, smelling the fumes from the coffee shop downstairs and pushing the things I knew around in my head, hoping they'd form a pattern I could recognize. It was late afternoon. I looked out my window at the boulevard below me. Nobody was frying eggs on the sidewalk. Off on another street somewhere a police siren wailed. They'd be busy in this heat. People got a little crazy in heat like this. Husbands began to ball their fists and frown at their wives. Meek, mousy-haired wives began to look at the breadknife and eye their husbands taking a nap in their undershirts and snoring, their throats exposed. In the barrio the prowl car boys would keep their hands a little closer to their guns. And in the hills where the stars lived, people would sit on patios looking at the lights twinkle in the steamy evening below them in the basin, and the sweat that beaded on the sides of cocktail shakers would trickle off and make a wet spot in their linen slacks. The heat played no favorites.

It got slowly dark while I sat there looking out at the baking city and thinking and not getting anywhere. The end of another perfect day. Nobody called. Nobody came in. Nobody cared if I died or bought a house in Encino.

21

The Rancho Springs Development Corp. was on the second floor over a gas station in a pale beige stucco building with the rounded shape of the Spanish Southwest that everyone south of Oregon thought was authentic native Californian. The building was on the main street in Rancho Springs next to a place that sold tacos and across the street from a general store where three desert rats in bib overalls sat out front in the thick heat and rocked and spat occasionally out onto the street. A big yellow tomcat with a torn ear sprawled on the bottom stair leading up to the Rancho Springs Development office and I had to step over him when I went up.

Inside at the only desk in the place was a young woman with a bad sunburn. It was bad enough so that she moved a little stiffly as she turned toward me when I came in. The desk at which she sat and the chair on which she was sitting was all there was in the office for furniture. On the floor beside the desk was a cardboard carton and in the carton were a number of manila file folders.

On the desk was a phone. That was it, there was nothing on the walls, no curtains on the windows. The room was as charming as a heap of coffee grounds.

I took off my sunglasses and smiled at the young woman. Her nose was peeling, and her pale hair was dry and bleached looking. She wore a flimsy white blouse with short sleeves and her thin arms were bright red.

"Dr. Bonsentir around?" I said.

She looked blank. She also looked pained and bored and tighter than a Methodist deacon.

"Who?"

"Dr. Claude Bonsentir," I said. "I was hoping to find him here."

"Never heard of him," she said.

She was chewing gum and her jaws moved slowly and with iron regularity on it. Occasionally she would open her mouth to stretch some of the gum into a thin grayish membrane with her tongue. Then her lips would close and the gum would disappear.

"This is Rancho Springs Development Corporation?" I said.

"Ann huh." She was busy with the gum.

"What exactly is it you develop?"

She tucked the gum away into some corner of her mouth and looked at me as if I had wriggled up from the kitchen drain.

167

"Listen, Jack," she said, "they hire me to sit here and answer the phone and take messages and if they want something typed I type it. You want to leave a message?"

"Who're 'they'?"

"Guys that run this place. Vinnie and Chuck."

"Vinnie and Chuck who?" I said.

She shook her head.

"You wanna leave a message?" she said.

"When you see Vinnie and Chuck," I said.

She got out a little note pad and a pencil.

"Yeah?" she said.

"Give them a big kiss for me," I said, and turned and went back out and down the stairs and over the cat and into the main street. The main street was maybe 100 yards long and didn't need to be, it only supported about six buildings. Between the buildings were vacant lots, mostly sand and a few weeds and here and there tumbleweed resting still in the windless heat.

I strolled down toward a gray, weathered clapboard building where a sign out front read RANCHO SPRINGS GAZETTE AND CHRONICLE. It was a single-storied storefront with a wide front window and a screen door. Inside was a counter running across the room. Behind it was a printing press and two desks.

A big woman in a man's white shirt and

gabardine slacks smiled easily at me when I came in. She wore her white hair short, and her face had the dark-tanned look of a desert person who spends a lot of time outdoors. She seemed in excellent health and fine spirits.

"Hello, stranger," she said. "Come to place an ad? Report something interesting? Either case this is the spot for it."

"Information," I said.

"Got that too," she said. "Name's Pauline Snow. Only thing in this godforsaken wasteland ain't hot is my name."

"Marlowe," I said. Guile hadn't done anything for me. I decided to try truth. "I'm a private detective from Los Angeles working on a case, and the name of the Rancho Springs Development Corporation has popped up in it."

Pauline Snow said "Humph," with a lot of feeling.

"I've been to the office and talked with the young woman who works there. I would have done better to talk with the cat, which doesn't chew gum."

"Rita," Pauline Snow said with as much feeling as she'd said *humph*.

"Yes," I said, "that's what I thought."

"Rancho Springs Development Corporation is a fancy name for a back-shanty operation

169

in which two bozos come in and start buying up any land they can get," she said. "You got a cigarette?"

I got the pack out and gave it to her, she shook one loose, put it in her mouth, gave me back the pack. I held a match for her. She took a long inhale and let the smoke out in two streams through her nostrils. She looked me over.

"Private eye, is it?"

I nodded modestly.

"Well, you got the build for it, I'll give you that."

"Why are they buying up land?" I said. "Is there something about Rancho Springs I'm missing?"

"Only thirty miles," she said, "east of Pasadena."

"Perfect for fans of the Rose Parade," I said. "Anything else?"

"I don't know, Marlowe. It doesn't make any sense at all. This is hardscrabble dry land. No farming, no industry, damned little of anything. A few people still prospect out here, and a few damn fools like me and my husband come out here thinking about clean air and freedom. Then the son of a bitch up and died on me and left me to run this paper myself for the last seven years."

"Thoughtless," I said. "Maybe Vinnie and

Chuck know something we don't."

"Vincent Tartabull and Charles Gardenia. They better for their sake, because right now they're holding a passel of the most worthless acreage God ever made."

"They local people?" I said.

"Hell no," Pauline Snow said. "They come in here about six months ago and rented that hole up over the gas station, which is pretty much a damn hole itself if you think about it, and hired that idiot Rita. And started buying land. Easy enough to do, nobody wants it, everybody's happy as hell to sell and get out. Most folks are here 'cause they can't sell."

"Know where they came from?"

"Los Angeles," she said.

"How do you know?"

"I used to be a reporter, Mr. Marlowe, for the Cleveland *Plain Dealer*. Now I'm just a fat old babe with no husband who runs a hicktown weekly in East Overshoe. But I haven't forgotten everything I used to know."

"I get the feeling, Mrs. Snow, that you haven't forgotten anything you used to know, and that you used to know a lot."

"You know how to make a girl feel right, Marlowe. You surely do."

"Anything else you can tell me about these guys?"

She shook her head. "Been trying to figure out their angle for a while," she said, "but I can't. It just doesn't make any sense."

"Know anybody named Bonsentir, Dr. Claude Bonsentir?"

"Sure. He's one of the names on the incorporation papers in the secretary of state's office."

I grinned at her. And nodded my head in mock homage.

"Happen to know his sock size?" I said. "Any identifying marks?"

"I'm not that good, Marlowe. I looked up the incorporation papers, like you probably did. Don't know more than that. They didn't tell me anything useful."

"No. They wouldn't. But I'm going to tell you something useful," I said. "There's some sort of connection between this outfit, the Rancho Springs Development Corp., and an outfit up in Neville Valley, called the Neville Valley Realty Trust."

"Neville Valley," she said. "Is that up north a ways, in the Mountains?"

"Yeah, about two hundred miles north of Los Angeles in the Sierra Nevadas," I said. "And you know what they're doing?"

"How the hell would I know that?" she said.

"It was a rhetorical question, Mrs. Snow.

They're buying up water rights."

She stared at me and opened her mouth and closed it and went and got a rolled-up map of California out of one of the file drawers near the printing press.

She unrolled it and spread it out on a desk top and bent over it, resting her hands on the desk, her head hanging as she pored over the map. After a few minutes she began to nod her head silently and kept nodding it as she rolled the map back up and put it away. When she returned to the counter she was still nodding.

"Gimme another smoke," she said.

I did. And a light. When she had her cigarette going and a lungful of smoke expelled she bent down behind the counter and rummaged around for a moment and came out with a bottle of rye whiskey and two glasses.

"We need to drink a little whiskey, I think, while we think about this."

I took the inch and a half she poured in one neat swallow.

So did she. She exhaled happily once and then poured two more drinks.

"You think they're going to run that water down from Neville Valley to here and make all that cheap desert land they bought worth a fortune?"

"They might," I said.

"Wouldn't that be something," she said.

"Problem is," I said, "the government's running some kind of land-reclamation project up there designed to do the same for Neville Valley."

"And you figure somebody's trying to steal it. The water."

"I don't know," I said. "I'm just trying to find one young woman, and everywhere I look things are peculiar and the case gets bigger and bigger."

"Well, maybe I can do some poking around at this end," she said. "You got someplace I can reach you?"

I gave her my card. She looked at the address. "Hollywood, isn't it?"

"Sure," I said. "Gumshoe to the stars."

"You know," she said, "what's funny. If we find out that everything is not, ah, kosher, in this deal. I mean, who the hell do you report a stolen river to?"

I drank the rest of my second drink and dried my mouth on the back of my first knuckle.

"Me, I guess," I said.

22

I had parked my car on the street across from the gas station above which the Rancho Springs Development Corp. had its rathole. When I got back to my car it was blocked by a black and white police car with a big silver star on the side. Around the circumference of the star were the words RANCHO SPRINGS POLICE.

Leaning against my car were two of Rancho Springs' finest. Probably all of Rancho Springs' finest. One was a long rangy leathery customer with a big walrus moustache. He wore a tan shirt and pants that had been laundered threadbare, and a big white ten-gallon hat with sweat stains around the base of the crown. There was a star pinned to his shirt, that said *Chief,* and he carried an old frontier-style .44 Colt in a scuffed leather holster which hung from a wide cartridge belt. The Colt must have had a barrel ten inches long. The other guy leaning on my car was probably six inches shorter than his chief and maybe a yard wider. He had no neck at all, his jowly red face rising directly from his shoulders, and his faded tan uniform shirt was stretched to its limit over his stomach, so that the buttonholes pulled, and in the gaps between the buttons the pallid skin showed through. He too wore a big hat and it succeeded in making him seem even squatter. Above his small eyes, his blond eyebrows were bleached pale and looked like white slashes against his red face. His silver badge said *Sergeant* on it. He had a government-issue .45 automatic in a military-style flap holster on a web belt that he wore tight, allowing his belly to hang over it.

"This your car?" the fat cop said.

"Nice huh?" I said. "You want to sit in it?"

"What the hell's that supposed to mean?" the fat cop said.

"Sorry," I said. "I didn't mean to talk so fast."

"You'll be talking fast in the back cell under the big lights in a little while," the fat cop said.

"The smaller the town, the tougher the buttons talk," I said.

The fat cop put his hand on his holster.

"You want to say that again, tough guy?" he said.

The chief put a hand like a catcher's mitt on the fat cop's shoulder.

"Now, Vern," he said mildly. "Got no

176

call getting yourself into some sort of rutting contest with this fella. Just deliver our message and help him on his way."

"I figured there'd be a message," I said.

The fat cop continued to glower at me, hand poised on his holster flap. I could have shot off his nose and put the gun away by the time he got unbuttoned.

"Smart fella," the chief said easily. "Could tell you were a smart fella, minute you showed up in town. Lotta smart fellas in the city, I guess. Don't get a chance to see many of them out here eating sand with us cactus rats."

"You actually hire this guy as a cop?" I said, and jerked my head at the fat cop, "or do you just keep him around for shade?"

"Vern's a handy fella. Does good work with a blackjack. But he ain't always as polite as he should be, I guess. What's the purpose of your visit to our town, Mr. Marlowe?"

"Did you get it off the registration?" I said. "Or did Rita give it to you?"

"Registration," the chief said. "Rita couldn't remember if you give her a name."

I nodded. There was a moment of silence.

"We asked you a question, city boy."

"I'm a private detective on a case," I said.

"What case?" the chief said.

"Confidential," I said.

The chief made a little nod of his head and the fat cop hit me on the right shoulder with a blackjack. The pain went the length of my arm and up into my head. The fat cop was very quick with his blackjack, I hadn't seen him take it out.

"He makes another move with that sap," I said to the chief, "and I'm going to feed it to him."

The chief made a small move with his right hand and the frontier Colt was in it and pointing up under my chin.

"Let's just all stop fiddling around with this thing," he said. "You out here asking questions about Rancho Springs Development Corporation. We don't like that. We don't like big-time hotshot city private detectives come weasling into our town and asking questions about our businesses. Vern here, he hates that especially."

"I guessed that," I said. The muzzle of the Colt was pressing firmly into the soft area under my jawbone.

"So we don't want you to do it no more, smart boy. We want you to get in your car and haul it out of Rancho Springs and not come back. 'Cause if you do come back we got a cell, way down back with no windows and one bright light where you and Vern can sort of cha cha cha until everything's clear. Comprende?"

"Yeah," I said. "I can follow that."

The tall chief turned my head toward the car with the muzzle of his Colt.

"Dust," he said.

My right arm was numb and throbbing. I could barely move it. I tried not to let it show. I opened the car door with my left hand, just as if I always opened it with my left hand, and got in and started up. The two cops got in their car and pulled up and I went past them and headed out of town. They followed me all the way to the town line and then U-turned and headed back toward Rancho Springs, leaving a low pall of dust behind them as they dwindled in the rearview mirror. Every day some new friends.

23

I woke up with an idea. I also woke up with one arm throbbing like a toothache, and some soreness left in my jaw, and a dull tenderness behind my ear. But mostly it was the idea. I remembered something Vivian had said about Simpson having a place in the desert. I rolled out of bed and called her while the coffee dripped.

"Oh, I don't know," she said sleepily. "Somewhere out past Pasadena."

"It got a name?"

"Springs, some kind of springs," she said. "I've never been there. I just know Daddy used to go out there when he was well."

"Rancho Springs?"

"That sounds right. Will I see you soon, Phil?"

"I hope so," I said, and hung up the phone. Phil?

I called Pauline Snow.

"Marlowe," I said. "Do you know if a guy named Randolph Simpson lives anywhere around Rancho Springs?"

"A guy named Randolph Simpson? Marlowe, where the hell have you been living the last thirty years? Randolph Simpson is not a 'guy.' That's like saying 'a guy named John D. Rockefeller,' for God's sake."

"Does he live there?"

"Sure. Everybody knows that."

"Do you have any access to him?"

"Of course not. No one has access to Randolph Simpson. Why?"

"I think he's hooked into the business with the water rights and the land development."

"Simpson?"

"Dr. Bonsentir is his doctor."

"That doesn't mean he is involved in some scheme."

"Few nights ago," I said, "a couple of hard numbers leaned on me pretty good on a rainy street in Hollywood. They told me to stay away from Randolph Simpson and Dr. Bonsentir."

"Because you were poking around in the water rights thing?"

"Because I have been looking for a young woman who went from Bonsentir's clinic to Simpson. The hard boys that poured it to me were driving a Buick sedan registered to the Neville Valley Realty Trust."

"The people buying water rights up north."

"Un huh."

"Doesn't prove Simpson's involved in it.

Could be just about the girl."

"Why are they driving a car registered to the Neville Valley Trust? And how much of a coincidence is it that Neville Valley seems to be connected to Rancho Springs, and Simpson has a place in Rancho Springs, and his doctor is on the board of the development company buying land in Rancho Springs?"

"Okay," Pauline Snow said. "You got a point. It's not something you can take to court, or even something I can print — yet. But it's something."

"How about Chuck and Vinnie," I said. "You have anything on them?"

"Just addresses," she said. "You want them?"

I did. She rummaged off the phone for a couple of minutes while I put some cream and sugar in my coffee and sipped it. Then she came back and gave me an address in Los Angeles.

"Business address, I assume," she said. "I don't know L.A. that well, but that sounds like downtown."

"It is," I said. "I'll go call on them. Anything you can find out about Randolph Simpson is welcome."

"What are we trying to do, Marlowe? Exactly?"

"How the hell do I know?" I said. "I was hired to find the girl. I guess we're trying to do that."

I had some toast and drank the rest of my coffee, and in an hour, with my arm still throbbing, but my head feeling better, I was headed downtown.

Gardenia-Tartabull Insurance and Real Estate was in a building on Bunker Hill near Fourth Street that had impressed everyone when they built it. It was less impressive now, but under the grime you could still see the glamour of its youth. The lobby was an open shaft to the roof through which the iron cage elevators went up and down, and around which a tier of filigreed iron balconies marked the floor levels. Gardenia-Tartabull was on the sixth floor behind a pebbled glass door that had NOTARY PUBLIC in small black letters under the name of the firm.

Inside, at a desk with nearly nothing on it, was a redhead with a lot of hair, wearing a tight green dress. She was tilted back in her chair with her legs crossed, working very carefully on getting her nails painted in a shade of flame to match her hair. I waited for a minute until there seemed a break in the process. She didn't look up.

I said, "Do you have another job here, or is that it?"

"Wait a sec," she said. Her forehead was wrinkled with concentration and the tip of her tongue showed between her bright lips. I hooked a straight chair from against the wall beside the door and turned it around and sat on it with my forearms resting on the back. I put my chin on my arms and watched her paint.

"How long does this usually take you?" I said.

She didn't answer, just shook her head and frowned a little harder as she put a smooth swipe of lacquer on the nail of her second finger. She had eight to go.

"You don't have to look up," I said. "And you don't have to speak. Just nod or shake your head. Is Gardenia or Tartabull in?"

She nodded. Her little nailbrush was poised over the second nail. It was clear that she could nod or she could paint her nails, but she couldn't do both.

"Tartabull?"

She shook her head.

"Gardenia?"

She nodded. I glanced around the room. There were four or five green metal file cabinets along the walls, and in the wall behind her desk were two doors, each with a pebbled glass window. One said CHARLES GARDENIA and the other said VINCENT TAR-

184

TABULL. I stood up.

"Thank you for your help," I said, and went past her desk toward Gardenia's office. She almost spoke then, but I had opened the door to Gardenia's office before she could and then it was too late. As I closed the door behind me I saw her lower her head again and stare at her nails.

Behind his desk with a copy of the Los Angeles *Times* spread out in front of him, munching a cruller, was the fat guy in the seersucker suit I'd seen getting out of the black Buick in the Neville Valley Trust parking lot up north. He had on the same suit. There was a cup of coffee on the desk beside the paper. A little spiral of steam drifted up from it. On the hand that held the cruller was a diamond pinkie ring. Gardenia gazed at me without expression while he finished chewing the bite he'd taken from his cruller. Then he took a sip of his coffee.

When he had swallowed the coffee he said, "Whaddya want?"

"My name's Marlowe," I said. It didn't seem to impress him. "I'm a private detective working on a case and I keep bumping into a couple of businesses, yours being one of them."

"And what do you think my business is?" Gardenia said.

"I know you do business as Rancho Springs Development Corporation."

"That right?" Gardenia said. He seemed a lot more interested in his cruller than in anything I had to say.

"And I know you are connected with the Neville Valley Realty Trust."

"Yeah?"

"Yeah."

I felt like I was in a second-feature movie. Gardenia finished his cruller, drank some more coffee.

"So what's this case you're working on?" he said.

"I'm looking for a girl."

"Is that all?" Gardenia said. "Hell, you can have the one out front, you want. She doesn't do me any damn good."

"Paints a nice nail though."

"Yeah." Gardenia rummaged in a paper sack and came out with another cruller. He took a bite and chewed it happily.

"So who's this girl you're looking for?"

"Carmen Sternwood, her father was General Guy Sternwood. Maybe you've heard of him. He was in the oil business."

Gardenia shook his head. "Nope. Can't say I have. How come you're looking around me? I don't know any broads that are missing."

"I think she's with Randolph Simpson."

"So?" Gardenia shrugged. "I don't know Randolph Simpson."

"He connected to Rancho Springs? He lives out there."

"What I hear, he lives a lot of places," Gardenia said. The conversation didn't interest him. He examined his hand where he'd held the cruller and licked a crumb off the index finger.

"A couple of hard boys in a car registered to Neville Valley Realty Trust stopped me on the street one night and told me to stay away from Randolph Simpson."

Gardenia shrugged.

"They told me to stay away from Dr. Bonsentir too. And not to look for Carmen Sternwood."

Gardenia dusted his hands off to get rid of any crumbs his tongue had missed. Then he leaned a little forward over his desk, and got a cigar out of a leather humidor and stuck it in his mouth and got a desk-top lighter going and lit the cigar.

"Look, what did you say your name was?"

"Marlowe."

"Well, Marlowe, I appreciate you got a problem. But to tell you the truth, it's not my problem, if you see what I mean, and I figure that I give it about all the time I owe it."

"You wouldn't just happen to know where

Carmen Sternwood is?"

"Marlowe, I give you an A for trying hard, but I don't know where she is, or who she is, or, for that matter, how she is. You think she's with this guy Randolph Simpson, then whyn't you chase over to his house and ask him about it."

I took a business card out of my pocket and laid it on his desk.

"I think you overplayed it a little with the *this guy Simpson* line," I said.

Gardenia shrugged and spread his hands. The palms were clean and pink and soft. The nails had been manicured and buffed.

"You think of anything, you might call me," I said.

"Sure thing," Gardenia said. He stood up heavily, his white shirt stretched very tight over his belly. He put out his hand.

"Thanks for stopping by."

I shook my head at his outstretched hand.

"I'm too old for horse crap," I said.

He didn't care. He smiled, sat back down, picked up his coffee cup and began to read the *Times* again, tracing a forefinger along the printed line while the cigar he held in the same hand sent its pleasant ribbon of smoke up toward the ceiling.

I left and didn't shut the door on my way out. Teach him a lesson.

24

Morris Isaacson had a law office with two secretaries in West Hollywood near the intersection of Horn and Sunset. He sat back in his big swivel chair and put his small feet on the desk and admired the polish on his shoes.

"Water rights," he said thoughtfully. "It's a Western term. East of the Mississippi they have riparian rights. Means anyone on the shore of a river, say, has limitless rights to the water in the river. West of the Mississippi, it being sorta dry out here, they have water rights in which people abutting a river have discrete rights, defined by how much of the land they own abuts."

"And you can sell those rights?"

"Buy or sell," Isaacson said. He had a thin gray moustache and slick silver hair and a strong nose. "Not riparian rights, they go with the land. But water rights, sure, they can be bought and sold."

"Anything illegal about it?"

"No more than any other transaction. Obviously there can be no intent to defraud, the usual rules apply. But there's nothing special about water rights."

"And if I bought up all the water rights to some river somewhere, then I could do whatever I wanted with the water?"

"Yep."

"Would the government buy water rights?"

"Sure, been doing it all over the West."

"Would they employ a private company to do it for them?"

"Marlowe, how the hell would I know? Far as I can tell, the government will do about anything at all."

I was silent.

"Not to be a kvetch, Marlowe, but sitting here watching you think isn't earning me any money. Explaining water rights to you hasn't earned me a hell of a lot either."

"I owe you," I said.

"I know you do," Isaacson said. "But you don't have anything to pay with. Maybe someday, I lose a client, I'll get it back."

I got up without comment and left. When I got back to my office the pasty-faced blond guy that walked behind Eddie Mars was sitting in the waiting room with his feet stretched out in front of him and his hat tilted forward over his face. I walked past him without comment and unlocked my inner office and opened the window to let the hot air in and sat behind my desk. In a minute he ambled in, tougher than two scorpions.

"Eddie wants you to come over to the club," he said. His lips barely moved when he spoke and he had to tilt his head back to see out from under his hat brim.

"So what," I said.

"It's about the Sternwood cookie," Blondie said.

"Which one?"

"Vivian. Eddie says you should come over. She's there. Somebody laid some knuckles on her."

"Who?"

"Eddie didn't say. Just said I should bring you."

"I'll bring myself," I said.

Blondie shook his head. "Eddie said I should bring you."

I stood up. "You want to bring me, you can start now. You'll think you walked into a propeller."

"Tough today," Blondie said.

"Tough, quick, and sick of almost everybody I've met this week."

Blondie shrugged. "Eddie didn't say anything about dropping you. See you at the club."

He turned around and walked out. I followed him a minute later and arrived at the Cypress Club ahead of him.

It looked shabbier in daylight, like clubs always do. The threadbare spots that indirect lighting concealed looked sadly real with the sun shining on them. The places where the paint had peeled in the steady Pacific wind stood out in clear relief in the daylight. Things seemed to look better in the shadows.

Mars was the exception. He looked just as good in daylight with a pearl-gray sport coat and a charcoal shirt with the collar points spilling out over the lapels. He was in the office with Vivian when I went in.

She didn't look good. Her upper lip was puffy and one eye was nearly closed with the darkening rings of a classic shiner developing. What makeup she may have had was worn away and her hair was messy and she looked haggard and frightened and vulnerable. And beautiful.

"What happened?" I said.

She looked at Eddie and he answered for her.

"She got a call from Bonsentir's clinic, told her Carmen was back and she should come up. She went instead of calling me. Up along Mulholland a couple of sluggers ran her off the road, tossed her around a little, and told her to put a leash on you."

"Or else?"

Mars nodded. His face was perfectly calm

192

but his eyes glittered.

"Leave it alone, Marlowe," Vivian said in a choked voice. "Leave it alone, get the hell out of our lives and let us have some peace."

"And what?" I said. "And let Carmen go wherever Bonsentir sends her and you do whatever two thugs tell you to do? That's peace?"

Vivian looked at Eddie and back at me.

Mars said, "He's right, sugar," in a voice so flat and cold it didn't sound human.

She stared at him for a moment and at me for a moment and began to cry. "Look at me," she said, "look at me." And she cried harder, but crying hurt her so she got it under control. Mars didn't say anything to her, but walked across the room and put an arm around her. She stood rigid.

"I called you," she said to me, fighting to keep her voice steady. "You weren't there. So I went and when this happened I came to Eddie."

"No explanations necessary," I said.

Mars was looking at me. I don't think he heard any of what was being said. The glitter in his eyes was like ice.

"What are we going to do about this, soldier?"

"Something," I said. "We in this together now?"

Mars nodded. "For now," he said. His

mind seemed far away. "Doesn't mean we're pals, soldier. Just means we got a common interest."

"Yeah," I said.

"What are you going to do?" Vivian said.

"Something," I said.

"Sugar, if you're all right, I'll send a couple of boys home with you," Mars said. "Marlowe and I have to talk."

"And I just sit by while you men decide my life," Vivian said.

"You got a better idea?" I said.

She shook her head and her battered face darkened again as if she were going to cry. But she didn't.

"No, dammit, it's how women have always lived. Stay home, wait, hope, while the men do 'something.' Maybe I'll get drunk."

"I'll have a couple of boys stay around you," Mars said. "Nobody's going to hurt you again."

"The hell they won't," Vivian said and turned and went.

Blondie appeared at the door as soon as she went through it.

"Take somebody, drive her home. Stay with her."

Blondie disappeared.

The club was silent, the way night places are in the day. Mars reached into a desk drawer and took out a short-barreled Colt .45 and put it on his desk. He put a box of shells beside it.

"You got a theory on all this?" he said.

I sat across the desk from him and crossed my legs and tossed my foot a minute.

"I figure Carmen's an accident." I said. "I figure the issue is some kind of trick that's happening between Neville Valley and Rancho Springs. Somebody's buying water rights up in Neville Valley where there's a government irrigation project in the works. And they're buying real estate in a place called Rancho Springs — which doesn't have any springs — in the desert east of Pasadena."

"You got a thought who that might be, soldier?"

"I'm getting to that," I said. "I figure that the plan is to divert the water from Neville Valley to Rancho Springs and get rich selling fertile land which they bought for nothing when it was dust bowl."

"Two hundred miles?" Mars said.

"Sure," I said. "I've done a little reading. The Los Angeles aqueduct runs that long, down from Owens Valley."

"So they buy cheap land, steal some water to fertilize it, and sell it expensive," Mars said.

I nodded. "I figure Bonsentir's in it, and

Simpson's in it. This kind of deal needs a lot of bankroll. And I figure they have bribed the government people doing the water development in Neville Valley, and I figure they own the law in Rancho Springs. Couple of desert cops chased me out of there the other day."

"People been sort of unfriendly toward you," Mars said.

"I'm used to it," I said. "So they have this sweet deal all locked up and under control and then I come along, Marlowe the snoop, looking for Carmen Sternwood and everyone has a swivet for fear that I'll stumble onto the Neville Valley scheme."

"So why didn't somebody just dump you?" Mars said. He took a silk show handkerchief out of his breast pocket, refolded it carefully, and put it back in his breast pocket.

"They thought they could scare me off. A murder attracts too much attention."

"So why didn't somebody give Carmen back? You say you think Simpson's got her," Mars said.

"Hard to figure that," I said. "It may have something to do with Simpson being such a twisted gee. He's so rich he may not think like you and me, Eddie."

"And he's wired," Mars said.

"Very," I said. "His protection has got

protection. I think he thinks he can do anything he wants without consequences."

"He can't beat up my girl," Mars said.

There wasn't anything there for me to talk about. I let it slide.

"Thing that doesn't fit is the murder. And maybe it doesn't fit, maybe it's just a random thing that's not connected to the rest."

"The hack murder?"

"Yeah. The Sternwood phone number was on a matchbook in her purse."

"I read about it," Mars said. "Didn't mention any names in the paper."

"Sternwoods got a little juice themselves," I said.

"You figure it was Carmen gave her the number?"

"I don't know. I don't know anything about the murder. I wish it weren't in here at all, it muddies everything up."

"A sweet deal like that," Mars said. "They're not going to let you push them off it."

"True."

"There's maybe fifty, maybe a hundred million dollars you could make in that kind of a deal."

"Yeah."

"They'll kill you if they have to," Mars said. "I would."

"It's been tried," I said. "One of yours tried."

Mars nodded thoughtfully.

"I don't care about you, soldier," he said. "But to take them off Vivian's back, we're going to have to bust this deal for them, I think."

"I think so," I said. "And we're going to have to find Carmen."

"Little Miss Hotpants," Mars said and shook his head. "You'd do her sister a favor if you buried her."

"Wasn't hired to do that," I said.

"Maybe you could be hired to forget it," Mars said.

"You know better, Eddie," I said.

"Yeah," he said. "You're not smart, soldier. But I'll give you that you're stubborn. So we find Carmen too."

I nodded. Me and Eddie Mars. Partners. A couple of pals. Two smart boys side by side. Mars and Marlowe. Marlowe and Mars. Had a nice ring to it. I felt like I ought to go home and gargle.

Which I did.

25

I was in my office, with my coat off and my tie down, drinking a shot of rye from a water glass and thinking about whether to have another one or go to dinner, when Bernie Ohls came in.

"Cocktail hour?" he said.

"Sure," I said. "I settle in, drink a couple of these, and tell myself about my day. It's very convivial."

"Want to come to the morgue and look at a body?"

"What could be nicer," I said.

Ohls had the siren on all the way downtown through the rush-hour traffic.

"Corpse in a hurry?" I said.

"What's the point of being a cop if you can't use the siren?" Ohls said. "It's the only fringe benefit."

The L.A. County morgue was cool and dim and pleasant on a hot day. Our footsteps were loud as we followed the attendant along the stacked rows of pull-out storage drawers, like filing cabinets for the dead. The body the morgue attendant pulled out was an old woman, with white hair, and her head twisted at an odd angle. It was an old woman I knew. Maybe she could see her house now.

"Mrs. Swayze," I said.

"She fit your description," Ohls said.

"Broken neck?"

"ME hasn't seen her yet," Ohls said. "But that's what it looks like."

"Where'd you find her?"

"Off the coast highway," Ohls said.

"Figure she was killed elsewhere and dumped?" I said.

"We don't know she was killed," Ohls said. "She could have fallen."

"Come on, Bernie," I said, "you been a cop too long to believe that. She's a patient at Resthaven, a witness in Carmen Sternwood's disappearance, when we want to question her she's gone. Now she turns up dead, the second person with a Sternwood connection to do so."

"Sure," Ohls said. "But I also been a cop long enough to wait for the coroner to tell me what he knows."

"And what about the sanitarium?"

"What about it? We got not one piece of evidence that Bonsentir's not clean as toothpaste. Two people he claims he discharged turn out to be problems — maybe. Can we close him down because of that?"

"He's dirty as hell," I said.

"Sure," Ohls said. "You know it and I know it. Can you convince a DA? A judge? A jury? You know the answer to that, Marlowe."

"Okay I put her away?" the morgue attendant said.

Ohls nodded. The drawer slid silently shut on an oiled track.

Ohls and I left her there and headed back outside where life was on going and the sun was the color of old brass in the late afternoon sky.

The traffic had thinned by then and Ohls left the siren off and let the car cruise with the traffic flow back toward Hollywood.

"Got something else for you to chew on, Marlowe," Ohls said.

I had my hat tilted forward over my eyes to keep the setting sun out, and was leaning back against the seat feeling older than Mount Rainier.

"Yeah?"

"Lola Monforte," Ohls said. "The dismembered stiff in the canyon."

"Yeah."

"Told you she used to be an actress, we turned up a guy used to be her agent. Says she was trouble, a boozer and a nympho."

"Something else?" I said.

"Said she spent some time at Resthaven, getting a few of the kinks straightened out."

I stayed perfectly still under my hat brim. Ohls and I were both silent. Ohls bore left at the V where Hollywood runs off of Sunset.

"We figure that's the Sternwood connection," Ohls said. "Pals, a little girl talk about their mutual hobby, 'call me, honey, when you get out,' she writes the number in a matchbook."

"I suppose she was cured and discharged too," I said.

"Surprise, surprise," Ohls said.

"And you're not going to close him down?" I said.

"We're kind of hoping you'll find us something, Marlowe, help us do that."

I felt something icy move in the pit of my stomach. Where was Carmen?

"Sure," I said from under my hat brim. "Glad to."

26

My building was empty and my office was dark. I sat alone in it nursing a drink, staring out the open window at the hot California night. Below me on the boulevard fast cars roared up and down The Strip, double-clutching sometimes to make the engines roar. The neon splashed its bright colors upward and across my office, making bright shifting patterns in the unlit room. Some of the patterns were bright red like blood splattering on my walls.

Everywhere I looked in this case there was Dr. Bonsentir, and lurking behind him, getting more sinister each time his shadow fell, was Randolph Simpson. Randolph Simpson, the man with the money, the man with the power, the man with the twisted sexual appetites. Carmen was supposed to be with him and I was supposed to get her back. After that it got tricky.

Simpson had to be involved in the water rights swindle. It was a swindle that took big money. It was a swindle that required a lot of people to be bought off, or scared off, or both. And it required a guy to run it that didn't worry about eight or ten thousand people up in the Neville Valley whose lives would dry up and blow away as a result of the swindle.

The smell of gasoline exhaust drifted up through my open window, and of food being fried. More faintly came the hint of hibiscus, and bougainvillea, and the acrid perfume of eucalyptus. And barely discernible, almost obliterated by the gasoline fumes and cooking smells, was the scent of the ocean to the west as it came lumbering in from Asia. I felt old and tired and gritty, as if I'd been wrestling in a gravel pit.

I thought about dinner. It had no appeal. I thought about Vivian with her face bruised and her soul tangled in the dark tragedy of her family, and about the way her lips had felt, and the way her body had arched so strongly toward me that night in her bedroom. And I thought about Rusty Regan, whom I'd never met and who had gone a long ways quite a while ago to the place where Lola Monforte had gone, and Mrs. Swayze. Was it a peaceful sleep, I wondered, or did they dream? And if they did, what dreams? Nightmares? And when I went to sleep the Big Sleep would I have nightmares too? If I did, one of them would be the day Carmen asked me to teach her to shoot the little gun I'd taken from her when she tried to send Joe Brody over.

I went back around the sump and set the can up in the middle of the bull wheel. It made a swell target. If she missed the can, which she was certain to do, she would probably hit the wheel. That would stop a small slug completely. However, she wasn't even going to hit that.

I went back toward her around the sump. When I was about ten feet from her, at the edge of the sump, she showed me all her sharp little teeth and brought the gun up and started to hiss.

I stopped dead, the sump water stagnant and stinking at my back.

"Stand there, you son of a bitch," she said.

The gun pointed at my chest. Her hand seemed to be quite steady. The hissing sound grew louder and her face had the scraped bone look. Aged, deteriorated, become animal, and not a nice animal.

I laughed at her. I started to walk toward her. I saw her small finger tighten on the trigger and grow white at the tip. I was about six feet away from her when she started to shoot.

The sound of the gun made a sharp slap, without body, a brittle crack in the sunlight. I didn't see any smoke. I stopped again and grinned at her.

She fired twice more, very quickly. I don't think any of the shots would have missed. There were five in the little gun. She had fired four. I rushed her.

I didn't want the last one in my face, so I swerved to one side. She gave it to me quite carefully, not worried at all. I think I felt the hot breath of the powder blast a little.

I straightened up. "My, but you're cute," I said.

Her hand holding the empty gun began to shake violently. The gun fell out of it. Her mouth began to shake violently. Her whole face went to pieces. Then her head screwed up toward her left ear and froth showed on her lips. Her breath made a whining sound. She swayed.

I caught her as she fell. She was already unconscious. I pried her teeth open with both hands and stuffed a wadded handkerchief in between them. It took all my strength to do it. I lifted her and got her into the car, then went back for the gun and dropped it in my pocket. I climbed in under the wheel, backed the car and drove back the way we had come along the rutted road, out of the gateway, back up the hill and so home.

Carmen lay crumpled in the corner of the car without motion. I was halfway up the drive to the house before she stirred. Then her eyes suddenly opened wide and wild. She sat up.

"What happened?" she gasped.

"Nothing. Why?"

"Oh, yes it did," she giggled. "I wet myself."

"They always do," I said. . . .

I got up and poured the rest of my drink down the sink and rinsed the glass. I turned back my cuffs and splashed cold water on my face and toweled dry. I went to the window and shut it and turned and left the office and went home to the Hobart Arms to try and sleep.

If I dreamed I don't remember.

27

When I got to my office in the morning,
my phone was ringing. When I answered,
it was Pauline Snow.

"Marlowe," she said. "I don't know if it
means anything but there's a desert rat out
here, says he's found a murder site near
Randolph Simpson's place. The old fool's
drunk most of the time, and I'm not sure
but what he sees things."

"What makes him think it's a murder site?"
I said.

"He says there's blood all over the place."

"Hang up and look out the window," I
said. "You'll see me parking my car."

When I got there, Pauline Snow had made
a pitcher of iced tea and we sat in the newspaper office and had some while she talked.

"I started looking into the Rancho Springs
Development Corporation, and into Randolph Simpson, since you seemed to think
he was involved somehow."

The tea had a wedge of lemon in it, and
a lot of ice. I added some sugar and waited
for it to dissolve and for the tea to become

clear again. The desert heat was like a substance that pervaded everything.

"So I asked around, just casual, you know. Anybody know anything about the Rancho Springs company? Anybody know anything unusual about Randolph Simpson? I have a lot of contacts in this town, ought to, been here half my damned life, and the word spread. First thing happened was Cecil came around. Cecil Coleman's the chief of police here. He wanted to know why I was asking questions, and I told him it was because I was in the newspaper business and that's what you did in the newspaper business. And he said he thought I better not ask any more questions. And I said I was thinking about doing an editorial about how the local police don't seem to arrest anybody except occasional speeders passing through. And he said I better not do that either. And we sort of jawed at each other for a while and then he left and said I'd be hearing from him."

"He's a bad enemy," I said.

"Marlowe, at my age, even an enemy is better than boredom."

"How about the murder site?" I said.

"Well, Shorty, that's the desert rat, he heard from somebody I was interested and he came in here and said he could tell me a story to put in the paper. So I gave him a shot of whiskey and he sat and told me that he was nosing around in an old deserted mineshaft — lot of desert rats do that, see if there might be a little dust left that got overlooked — and he found a sort of room a little ways in, really just a widening of the shaft, probably, that was splashed all over, he says, with blood. According to Shorty the whole room was covered with dried blood. So I thought I better let you know. As I say, it may be nothing. . . ."

"Shorty talk to the cops?" I said.

"He says no, and I believe him. People like Shorty get pretty short shrift from Cecil."

"And Vern," I said.

"You've met them?"

"Yeah. Where is this mineshaft?"

"Southeast of town," Pauline said. "I'll drive you."

"You don't need to," I said.

"I used to be a crime reporter, Marlowe. I've seen blood. It doesn't scare me."

"Scares me," I said.

She had a Ford pickup and she drove it far too fast for the roads. Or maybe it was right for the roads and too fast for me. I decided it didn't matter. We went southeast out of town through the flat hot land. There was tumbleweed, and occasionally a saguaro cactus looking somehow regal in the still desert air. The road was unpaved and soon became merely two wheel ruts as the pickup jounced and rattled along.

The mineshaft went horizontally into a low rise about two hundred yards off the road. The entrance was shored with timbers and the rubble of mine dross fanned out from the entrance for maybe fifty yards. There were the faint indentations of wagon wheels leading from the mine entrance toward the road, and the only sound I heard as we walked toward the mine was the desert wind that swept almost unimpeded over hundreds of miles and scattered the grit around the entrance, and pushed the tumbleweed along. Inside the mine entrance the sound of the wind turned into a hollow tone a little like a train whistle, but nowhere near as loud. Pauline Snow turned on the big battery lantern she'd brought and we walked, our feet crunching, through the litter of the shaft floor for maybe twenty feet where it turned a little and widened before it started to descend. The walls and gravel floor were crusted with blackened blood. I could smell it, no longer rich as it must have been when it was fresh, but still the lingering unmistakable scent of it. Blood had splashed on the walls, and ran in thick puddles on the floor where it had coagulated around the small scatter of stones. I heard Pauline's breath go in.

"Maybe you should stay with the truck," I said.

"No."

The light moved slowly as she panned the room. On one wall at about shoulder height a bloody handprint stood in black outline to the reddish stone of the shaft. There were drip lines where blood had spattered and run slowly down the walls.

I squatted on my haunches and looked closely at the dried pools, the surface faintly glossy in the lantern light. I was always amazed at the amount of blood there was in a human body. Among some rocks the size of footballs something metallic gleamed.

"Over there," I said, and Pauline flashed the light where I pointed. I went over and picked up a surgical saw. I handled it carefully, although the chance of useful fingerprints was about equal to the chance of a genie popping out of the mineshaft and telling us what happened. I moved slowly over the floor of the room. Among some other rocks, further back in the shaft, I found a scalpel. I was careful with it, too. There was nothing else to find in the murder room, we went a little further down the shaft and saw no sign of anything having been before us. We went back to the blood room.

"What do you think?" Pauline Snow said.

"I think I know where Lola Monforte was cut up," I said.

"The dismemberment murder in L.A.?"

"Yeah."

"You think it happened here?"

"Yeah. Where's Simpson's place from here?"

We were walking back out of the shaft. I carried the surgical saw and scalpel.

In the daylight I could see the manufacturer's name engraved on the blade near the handle, where the blood hadn't covered it. *Williamson Surgery* it said. I took a deep breath of hot desert air trying to get the faint smell of old blood out of my lungs.

"We may be on Simpson's place," Pauline said. "He owns two thirds of everything out here."

"Can we take a look?" I said. "At some of the more settled parts?"

"Sure."

We walked back to the truck. I put the saw and the scalpel behind the front seat and we went back out to the wagon ruts and headed east. In maybe twenty minutes we came to a paved highway.

"It's Simpson's," Pauline said. "Runs up

and connects to the interstate. He had it built for him."

"Anyone would," I said.

We drove south on the highway for another fifteen minutes and there ahead of us rising from the desert was something from Scheherazade. Three stories with turret, made of stucco, surrounded by a high stone wall off of which the sun glittered.

"No moat?" I said.

"Maybe inside," she said. "I don't know."

When we were close enough I could see the broken glass set in the top of it. There were the tops of trees showing above the walls, which meant there was water in there. The house and the walls were in a faded pink tone that probably looked rose in the hot desert sunset. Pauline parked a hundred yards or so away from the citadel and left the motor running. For the first time since I'd met her, including the trip down the mine-shaft, she looked frightened.

"Simpson doesn't welcome company," I said.

"No."

The complex of Simpson's desert retreat seemed to be the size of a medium city. Beyond the walls was a runway for, no doubt, Simpson's private plane. There was barbed wire around that, and around the cluster of outbuildings that gathered at the far end of the runway.

"It's best not to stay long," Pauline said. She was unconsciously revving the truck motor as we sat.

"Hard to get in there," I said.

"Hard? My God, Marlowe, it's impossible. You'd have to have an army."

The walls were too high to see into the citadel. From where we were there was no sign of movement. But Carmen Sternwood was probably in there. Sucking her thumb, giggling, and maybe, now and again, for old times' sake, throwing a wingding.

For all I knew she liked it in there. For all I knew Randolph Simpson was her dream man. For all I knew he'd been Lola Monforte's dream man too.

"We got to get out of here, Marlowe," Pauline said.

I said "Sure," and she spun the truck in a gravel-spinning U-turn and headed back away from Simpson's bastion, faster than we'd come.

28

We were back in Pauline Snow's office and I was on the phone with Bernie Ohls.

"That's San Bernardino County," Ohls was saying. "I'll get someone from the San Berdoo DA to go down and take a look."

"And a blood sample?"

"Now there's an idea," Ohls said. "And we could even compare it to Lola Monforte's, see if they were the same type."

"You're lucky to be dealing with a trained professional."

"Come in and see me when you get back to Los Angeles," Ohls said and hung up the phone.

"I left you out of it," I said to Pauline Snow.

"I don't mind being in it."

"You will if some of Simpson's boys stop by, or the Rancho Springs police force, which is probably saying the same thing."

"I told you before, Marlowe. I'm too old and fat to be scared. Besides, they'll want to know how you found the mineshaft, and what I know about cops, they won't be satisfied with you not telling."

"What I think is you should go stay with someone, away from here, until this is over."

She shook her head. "No," she said. "I'm in, and I'm here. For the duration."

The someone from the San Berdoo DA's office turned out to be two plainclothes dicks and a technician type. We all trooped out to the shaft and the dicks talked to us while the technician meditated over the death scene. I gave them the saw and the scalpel and they told me that I shouldn't be tampering with evidence and I told them that I agreed. That it would have been better to leave them around and let someone take them away. And they said they didn't need a smart punk from Los Angeles to take care of evidence for them, and I said that it didn't matter where the smart punk came from as long as there was one, and we got along famously. One of the dicks was a big sandy-haired guy with freckles and humorous eyes who looked like he might have sampled a drink now and then.

"You going to coordinate with the Rancho Springs police?" I asked him.

He grinned and looked at his partner, a dark slender cop named Hernandez.

"We going to coordinate with Cecil, Manny?"

The dark cop shook his head. He didn't seem to have much to say, and his sandy-haired partner appeared to think he had to make up for that.

"Manny says no," he said. "Manny don't say, but probably thinks, that Cecil is some sort of cat vomit, and we don't coordinate parking violations with him, never mind maybe a homicide."

"I got no argument with that," I said.

They took down statements from us, and looked blank at the mention of Randolph Simpson, and told us to be available if they needed us. Then we went back to town and the San Berdoo boys went back to San Berdoo.

"Be very careful," I said to Pauline Snow. "This thing is bigger and uglier than any of us could have known."

"I'm not in danger now," she said. "Too many people know what I know. No point to killing me. Hell, the San Bernardino DA knows it now."

"True," I said, "but these are vicious people. And you're alone."

She reached into a drawer in her desk and came out with an old frontier Colt.

"Not entirely," she said.

I drove back to Los Angeles in the late afternoon with the sun in my eyes most of the way. To the north the mountains were sere and lifeless. As I drove through Pasadena I could see the Rose Bowl far down to my right. Ahead was the San Fernando Valley, green and precisely parceled. I knew Simpson had killed Lola Monforte. I didn't know it in ways that could be proved yet, but I knew it. I knew in the same way that Lola Monforte had been at Resthaven and been passed on to Simpson, just as, when he had tired of Lola, Carmen Sternwood had been passed on to Simpson. I was hoping that he hadn't tired of her yet. I knew Simpson and Bonsentir were partners in the Neville Valley water deal. Marlowe the super sleuth. Knows all, proves nothing.

I swung down on North Figueroa Street, through Highland Park, and on through Elysian Park onto Sunset, and west past hamburger stands and pink stucco places that sold hot dogs, and mortuaries made to look like mission churches, and fancy restaurants made to look like Greek temples or French country inns. Here and there a modest stucco house, or a shingle house, with a deep wide front porch, popped out among the rest of the junk and reminded me that people lived here too, not often, but just often enough to remind you of how it once was when Los Angeles was a comfortable sleepy place relaxing in the sun.

It was late in the day when I got to Hollywood and there was nothing left to do but go home and think about all the things I couldn't prove until I fell asleep. Which I did.

29

I dreamed all night of a blood-red room and woke up in the morning feeling like I hadn't slept. The morning was barely brighter than the night had been. The heat was still oppressive and thunder made guttural sounds above me as I stared out my open window. In the Hollywood Hills to the north, lightning flickered, and I could feel the hard rain waiting behind the hills, out over the San Fernando Valley. Again the thunder, closer this time, and the shiver of hot lightning came more quickly behind it.

I went to the kitchen to make coffee and as I measured it into the filter the rain came like a heavy wind rushing down. I went to the open window but the rain was coming straight down in an unwavering cascade and there was no need to close the glass. Below me on Franklin Avenue the rain hitting the hot pavement made steam that hovered low over the street. Puddles were forming and the few people on foot on the street were running for cover, newspapers or purses held over their heads. The foliage was already greening, glistening darkly in the rain which hissed down from clouds that seemed piled just above the rooflines. I couldn't see the hills anymore. The rain was too dense and the sky too low, except when the lightning slashed, close now, nearly simultaneous with the thunder.

I had breakfast, put on a trench coat, and went to work. The temperature had dropped, probably thirty degrees, and the rain had settled into a steady downpour that promised to last the day and maybe more. At mid-morning the headlights glowed on cars, and the lights in houses were on, showing bright through the windows in the general murk. I went west on Franklin, dropped down to Sunset on Highland, and took Laurel Canyon up to Mulholland, squinting as I went, through the rain that threatened to overmatch my wipers. The inside of my car was dense with humidity, but I didn't care. I had a plan. I couldn't get at Simpson, I couldn't prove he'd done anything illegal; though it's hard to get rich in this big wide wonderful country and not do something illegal. I didn't even know where Simpson was, inside which fortress, behind which wall. But I knew where Dr. Claude Bonsentir was, and I knew he was connected to Simpson and maybe if I watched Bonsentir long enough, the connection would show itself. Maybe he'd lead me to Simpson. Maybe Simpson would come to him. Maybe an MGM talent scout would see me sitting there and offer me a contract. It wasn't a hell of a plan, but it was the only one I could think of, and it was better than staying home and playing chess against myself from a book of problems.

I had to fight the car up Laurel Canyon, the road curved in a series of nearly hairpin turns as it rose up from the lowlands on the Hollywood side, and with the road slipperier than the pathway to damnation, and the traffic in the other direction crowding in to keep from sliding into the canyon, it was no drive for sissies.

I looped up over Mulholland Drive, carefully, and came back down Coldwater Canyon and parked on the road above Resthaven, partly shielded by a growth of azaleas, where I could look down at the sanitarium and watch. And watch. And take a nip from a pint of bonded rye I had in the glove compartment. And watch. And smoke a cigarette and take another nip of rye, and watch. And get my pipe loaded and burning just right and open my window a crack to let a little of the steam and smoke escape, and watch. That was the first day. The second day I did the same things. It still rained. I watched. They fought the Peloponnesian wars. They built the Acropolis, and the Roman forum, and I had another tap on the pint of rye and watched. In the afternoon things dragged. About midmorning on my third day of watching, the rain dwindled away and by noontime the sun had come out, but it was a gentle sun. The heat was gone, and the dripping landscape was being slowly dried by an easy breeze that moved in from the Pacific. My pint of rye was down to maybe an inch in the bottom of the bottle when Dr. Bonsentir came out of the front door of his sanitarium with the Mexican and the beachboy and went to a big black Cadillac that was parked there and got in the back. The Mexican got in the passenger's side in front and the beachboy got behind the wheel and off they went with me drifting along behind them. Tailing somebody alone is not easy, and if they are looking for a tail it's not really possible for long. But Bonsentir and friends seemed unconcerned and innocent as they headed down Coldwater and swung west on Sunset. I hung back two or three cars when I could and changed lanes frequently to put myself in different places in the rearview mirror. If they made me they showed no sign of it. We went straight out Sunset past the mansions and the rolling lawns and the high ornamental fences. Past the lawn statuary and the private entrances with private security where movie stars and name directors hid behind the wealth their houses flaunted, and did the things that everyone does when they are alone and have no need for pretense.

We swung south along the coast highway through Bay City. The Pacific danced in toward us today. Scrubbed clean by the rain, it sparkled in the new sun and unrolled itself luxuriously on the clean white beach. Bay City loomed above us on the left, fresh washed after the recent rains but tawdry still in the way only beach towns can get tawdry, full of false promise with the paint peeling off it in the salt air. Ahead of me the Cadillac headed steadily south, and the beach towns slid by us. Manhattan Beach, Hermosa Beach. A little south of Redondo Beach, near Palos Verdes, we went off the highway at a slant and curved around some scrub cedar and beach growth toward the water. I dropped back and crept down behind them. As I came around the last curve I saw the Cadillac pull into a space on a concrete apron that fronted on a pier. There was a white painted shack on the pier. The pier itself jutted straight out into the ocean, and a couple of kids sat on the landing with lines in the water. I cruised on by the pier where the Cadillac was parked and drove back up the looping drive that connected with the highway. As soon as I reached the highway I parked on the shoulder and hot-footed it back down toward the pier and stood in a screen of coarse and twisted cedar growth to watch.

I felt out of place and a little clumsy in my city suit and shoes. The sand shifted under my feet as I moved, and the wind off the water tossed the cedar limbs where I stood. The Cadillac sat where it had parked, its motor idling, the windows rolled up. No one got out. No one did anything that I could see. I shifted occasionally from one foot to the other, got out a cigarette, and lit it in the wind on the third try, cupping the match in my hands and shielding it by turning my back into the breeze.

The two boys sitting on the dock didn't catch anything. A single sea gull circled hope-fully over them, waiting. A couple of hundred yards out to sea, several smaller seabirds, gray with white chests, skimmed the surface of the waves, dipping occasionally to capture a small something and then, back in forma-tion, continued on, staying close to the foam crests.

At about two-thirty in the afternoon, a

boat edged up over the horizon. By three o'clock it was directly offshore, maybe 500 yards. It was, loosely speaking, a yacht. And the Empire State Building is, loosely speaking, a skyscraper. It was probably 400 feet long and had at least three decks. There were two smokestacks raked, and the whole thing was painted a bright, brand-new vanilla color. At the stern in blue letters was the name, RANDOLPH'S RANGER. As I watched they lowered a speedboat from two derricks on the stern and some guy in a sailor suit the color of the yacht clambered down a ladder and got in. There was a moment while he tinkered with the controls and then there was the faint hint of a roar and the boat swooped away from the yacht in a wide curve, leaving a broad rolling wake behind it as it headed for the pier. As it got closer I could hear the throb of its big engine.

Dr. Bonsentir got out of the backseat of the Cadillac. The Mexican got out of the front seat and the two of them began to walk toward the pier. The speedboat pulled in against the landing and the boy in the sailor suit held it there. It bobbed gently while Bonsentir and the Mex walked down the ramp and onto the landing. The Mexican handed Bonsentir in and hopped in himself as lightly as if his knuckles didn't drag on the ground, and the boy in the sailor suit spun the wheel expertly and the speedboat headed back toward *Randolph's Ranger.* The beachboy backed the Caddy up and turned it around and drove on up past me toward the highway. He had on big sunglasses and was too busy checking how he looked in the rearview mirror to notice me in the bushes.

The speedboat pulled up to the side of the yacht where a boarding ladder had been lowered and Bonsentir and the Mex went aboard. The speedboat eased around to the stern.

When the Caddy was out of sight I headed down toward the shack on the pier. From behind the bushes I had seen the telephone line running down to it. The guy that ran the shack had straggly white hair and a big belly pushing at his undershirt. His skinny arms were badly sunburned as were his shoulders where the undershirt exposed them. One of his front teeth was missing and he smoked a thin brown cigarette, hanging from the corner of his mouth. Half an inch of ash had accumulated on the cigarette.

I said, "Use your phone?"

He said, "It ain't a pay phone. It's a private phone."

"Doesn't mean you can't get paid for its use."

"Where you want to call?" he said.

"Local," I said. "Las Olindas."

"That ain't a local call," he said.

I took a ten-dollar bill from my wallet. "This cover it, you think?"

I could see the grayish tip of his tongue as he touched his lips with it near where the cigarette smoldered. The movement dislodged the ash and it fell onto his undershirt. He brushed it absently while he looked at the ten.

"Yeah," he said. "I guess that'll be okay if you don't talk long."

"Okay if I pause to take a breath?"

He took the ten and stuffed it unfolded into the side pocket of his khaki pants and walked to the door of the shack and leaned on the doorjamb with his back to me. That was supposed to give me privacy. I dialed the Cypress Club and got Eddie Mars.

"Marlowe," I said. "I'm down around Palos Verdes on a pier maybe ten miles south of Redondo, and I think I've found Simpson."

"He going to stay put?"

"I don't know, he's on a yacht about a quarter mile offshore. Right now it's anchored."

"Stay there, soldier," Mars said. "I'll come down."

"You got a boat?" I said.

"I can get one," Mars said.

"Good," I said. "Hold on."

I got off the phone. "What's the name of this place?" I said.

The geezer at the door turned, trying to look startled, like I'd interrupted his thoughts.

"This place?"

"Yeah. I'm giving my friend directions."

"Fair Harbor," he said.

I repeated it to Mars.

"Sit tight, soldier, I'm on my way."

"I'll be here, Eddie, inflating my water wings."

Mars hung up and so did I. Through the window of the shack I could see the speedboat pull away from the yacht again and head in toward the pier. I turned back and leaned on the counter, letting my jacket fall open so the geezer could see my gun.

"Listen," I said. "Name's Armstrong, undercover, U.S. Government. I can't give you details, but we're onto something big involving that yacht out there and I don't want you to mention anything about that phone call."

The geezer's eyes fastened on the gun butt under my coat. And he thought about the tenspot in his pocket.

"Sure thing." He nodded his head hard up and down. "Sure thing, Captain. Hell, I was regular Navy for ten years. You can count on me."

"Good," I said. Then I added, "Mum's the word," because I'd always wanted to say it and I was never going to get a better chance. The geezer nodded vigorously again, and I went and leaned against the doorjamb and tried for that bored efficient tough-guy look that G-men affect.

The speedboat curved in to the pier and the sailor boy cut the throttle and let it drift expertly in against the landing. When he had it moored he hopped out and came up the pier toward the shack. He was a big one, and tough looking with big hands and a coiling blue sea serpent tattooed on his right forearm. He looked at me hard. I stepped aside to let him pass and he went on into the shack.

"Need some ice," he said to the geezer.

"Yes, sir," the geezer said. "Got it right outside in the freezer. Ten-pound block? Twenty?"

"Two twenties," the sailor boy said. "Load 'em into the speedboat."

"This is, ah, usually cash and carry," the geezer said.

"Fine. I give you cash and you carry the ice down to the boat," the sailor boy said. There was a pause and then the geezer said,

"Sure thing" and came out of the shack and went around to the big icebox on the ocean side. Sailor boy ambled out after him and stood near me leaning his back against the shack while the geezer got out tongs and a rubberized shawl and carried the ice down to the speedboat.

"Nice breeze," the sailor boy said.

"Aye," I said.

"Do any sailing?" he said.

"No."

"From around here?"

"You with the census bureau?"

"Hey, pally, I asked you a civil question."

"I love being called *pally*," I said. "Almost as much as I like being asked civil questions."

"It wouldn't be a good idea to get too wise with me, pally."

"The hell it wouldn't," I said.

Sailor boy thought about it for a while and decided it wasn't worth the time. He shrugged and sauntered off down the pier to his boat. He sat in it while the geezer struggled down with the second block of ice, then he cranked it up and left the dock at full throttle, heading back toward the yacht.

The geezer came back up from the landing. His face was red and he was puffing.

I gave him a nod and a conspiratorial wink. He went on inside the shack. I waited. I'd been doing a lot of that lately. I hadn't done much of anything else lately, except occasionally to get whacked with a sap or threatened with a gun. Counting the ten I'd given the geezer to use his phone, I was at least nine dollars in the hole on this job. It wasn't the way to get rich.

Five hundred yards away, *Randolph's Ranger* rode quietly at anchor, moving very slightly with the slow swells out beyond the surf line. The answers to a lot of questions rode out there on the swells. Maybe Carmen Sternwood, five hundred yards away, cute as a ladybug but far dumber, with the moral sense of an hyena. And here's Marlowe to the rescue. And Randolph Simpson, whom I'd never met but who appeared to be a mutilation murderer and a thief on a monumental scale, not to mention Bonsentir, and his Mexican and probably six pit vipers. A fine group, can't wait to join you. Perfect company. Marlowe the all-purpose guest, fits in easily with murderers and psychopaths, friend to all, close associate of Eddie Mars, gambler, gunman, all-around crook. The sky and sea were taking turns being bluer and the sun skipping off the whitecapped onshore waves made the air seem effervescent. A small yacht, a ketch, came around the point to the south and pulled in close to the shore and dropped anchor. A slender girl with a smooth tan and very blonde hair got into the dinghy they were towing and rowed toward shore. She had on white shorts and sneakers and a blue and white striped top and her sunglasses were so big they covered half her face. On the deck of the ketch I could see a blond young man dressed about the same, coiling the excess anchor rope and furling the mainsail. The girl bought some ice and a loaf of bread and other sundries and came back out carrying the purchases in a brown paper bag. The geezer nearly fell over himself carrying the ten-pound block of ice down to the dinghy for her. Her legs were perfectly smooth and the color of good sherry. She flashed a smile at the geezer that would have melted the ice if he'd still been carrying it. He made a ridiculous snaggle-toothed smile back, and she cast off from the landing and rowed back to her boat with short effortless strokes. The geezer and I both watched her until she was back aboard and the mainsail went up. The ketch moved slowly on, up the cove and around the point north of us and out of sight. We were alone again. Me, the geezer, and *Randolph's Ranger*.

30

The two kids gave up on the fish and left. I watched them go, arguing with each other about who had the most near misses.

Eddie Mars showed up about twenty minutes later. He had on a heavy white turtleneck sweater and a long-billed boating cap. Blondie was with him, looking especially pale and citified in the salt air and sand of the cove. He wore sunglasses and a tan garbardine windbreaker. They parked the long black car on the pier and walked out toward the shack where I was homesteading.

"Simpson out there?" Mars said with a nod toward the yacht.

"I'm betting he is," I said.

"I'm a gambling man myself," Mars said. "Got a boat coming."

"How soon?"

"Be patient, soldier, takes a little while. Let's all just settle back here in the sun and sip something cold."

Blondie went into the shack and bought some ginger ale and went to the car and got a pint of good bourbon and brought it back and we poured it into paper cups that the geezer provided and added ginger ale and had a drink. The geezer looked at it like a drowning man eyes a lifeguard, but Mars ignored him.

"I spent a little time thinking about how you found this place," Mars said, "and I figure you had to be tailing Bonsentir."

"Yeah."

"How long you been on him?"

"About three days," I said.

"No help?"

"No."

Mars shook his head and grinned. His grin had all the warmth of a pawnbroker examining your mother's diamond.

"Got to hand it to you, soldier. You work at it."

I had nothing much to say to that, so I let it pass and sipped a little of the bourbon and ginger ale. Out around the yacht some gulls rode easily on the waves, waiting for something to turn up. We sipped our drinks. Blondie made us a second one. We sipped some of that. Around the point from the north came a big cabin cruiser with a flying bridge and a swordfishing rig off the prow.

"That's us," Mars said.

It was no more noticeable than a crocodile in a bathtub.

"Be no problem sneaking up on them," I said.

"It's not that easy," Mars said, "to come up with a boat on short notice. This one belonged to a guy used it to smuggle before he got old. Got a lot of engine."

The cabin cruiser churned in past *Randolph's Ranger* and slid up alongside the float at the foot of our pier.

"All aboard," Mars said and finished his drink. We went on down the pier and down the ladder and onto the cabin cruiser. It was old, but it was well kept. The brass was polished and the teak and mahogany gleamed with years of hand-rubbing. At the wheel was a tall leathery specimen with a straw hat tilted way forward over the bridge of his nose. He held the boat easily against the landing float while we climbed on board. On board with him was the pug with the clubbed ear and broken nose that I'd seen before, and three other hard-looking characters that I didn't know. None of them looked like fishermen. Mars nodded at the helmsman and he eased the boat away from the pier with a deft movement of his hand. We were barely idling as the boat moved back toward the yacht.

"You got a plan, soldier?" Mars was leaning on the rail with one hand in his pants pocket, thumb out, manicured nail gleaming.

"We should sit offshore a little and wait. If they move we'll follow them. Otherwise, when it gets dark I'll go aboard."

"Alone?"

"Yeah. We all go aboard and it'll be a gunfight and I don't want Carmen caught in the middle."

"She'd love it," Mars said, staring out at the water. "She'd giggle and suck her thumb and probably wet herself."

"I wasn't hired to get her shot."

"How much do you go for?"

"This job, a dollar."

Mars laughed.

"Well, you earn your money, soldier."

"Yeah. I can't wait to invest it."

"How you planning to get over to the yacht?" Mars said.

I nodded toward the skiff, stored upside down on the foredeck.

"I figure someone can row me over."

"And they'll pipe you aboard?"

"Maybe they won't notice," I said. "Let's find out."

Mars shrugged.

"Keep the yacht in sight," he said to the helmsman in the hat. Then he went back to looking at the horizon. We idled south of the cove and hung off the point, staying steady against the wind. The yacht stayed put and the day dragged on, the minutes dawdled by like reluctant schoolchildren. Mars studied the horizon. I studied the yacht. The guy in the hat kept the bow into the wind, and the rest of the crew played cards. Marlowe and the pirates.

From where we rested, I had a good view of *Randolph's Ranger*. The landing float at the back was still out, and the speedboat rode at a short tether beside it. It didn't look like they were going anywhere soon. On the deck occasionally a figure in white moved, circling the deck slowly without any apparent mission. All the action was below-decks.

The minutes continued to crawl past, pushing huge boulders ahead of them. The sun remained overhead it seemed forever, making no movement toward the west, getting no closer to the rim of the Pacific, hovering overhead while I waited.

Once, late in the afternoon, the speedboat made a wake-curling run back into the shack for more ice, but that was all. The gulls bobbed patiently on the dull blue water. We hung motionless, in suspended animation, off the southern point of Fair Harbor until finally, as I was about to pass my ninety-fifth birthday, the sun disappeared, in fact quite suddenly, behind the horizon and darkness began.

When it was as dark as it was going to get, we got the skiff into the water and Blondie got in to row me across.

"He'll wait around, near where he puts you aboard," Mars said. "He'll be there when you're ready to come back."

"Can he row?" I said.

Blondie paid no attention to me. He was in the skiff with his hands resting on the oars.

"Blondie's good," Mars said. "Don't underestimate him."

"Sure he is, so am I. I'll go over, dance two numbers with Simpson, and be back with Carmen. They'll think pirates boarded."

"How long before we come in and get you?" Mars said.

"Use your judgment. But give me some time. Simpson has a private army everywhere he travels and you may not have enough firepower."

Mars smiled his bleak smile at me.

"We'll see, soldier. We'll see."

I climbed down into the stern of the skiff and Blondie pulled easily on the oars and we slid quietly over the dark still water toward the yacht.

31

It was not as dark as I would have liked. The stars were bright and a nearly full moon loomed over the black water and the motionless yacht. Blondie pulled the skiff expertly up against the landing platform. I could hear the faint sounds of what sounded like it might be revelry, though it could have been an ax murder in progress. The voices were indistinct. The calm water lapped gently against the hull of the yacht. I could hear nothing else. No sounds of sentries on the deck. I stepped out of the skiff onto the float, and Blondie pulled away without comment. I felt the reassuring weight of the gun in my shoulder holster, then moved softly up the ladder toward the deck. It was a balmy night, with just enough coolness stirring off the ocean to make everything fresh. The deck seemed empty when I stepped on it, but I knew I had seen someone in a sailor suit earlier, and I stayed motionless behind a bulkhead and listened. Only the sound of the water and the faint human voices from below. I waited. The rigging creaked faintly. Looking off toward Mars' cabin cruiser, I saw nothing. It was sitting with no lights, behind the point. I couldn't see Blondie in the skiff. From below I heard kind of a pealing giggle, much higher pitched than the other sounds, that had a chilling quality to it, like the shriek of someone wailing for her demon lover. Carmen! On deck suddenly I heard the gentle scuff of feet wearing sneakers. And then I saw him, in a white sailor suit, wearing a web belt, with a regulation sidearm. Just like the real Navy except for the sneakers. A little sleepy, bored with the endless circuit of the boat, he went by me without seeing me and continued on along the deck toward the bow. I went aft toward a hatchway and reached it and was inside, quicker than the passing of youth.

Below, the sound of people talking came more clearly, and I could hear the clink of tableware. I went down another step, and then another, until I could see the corridor that ran, apparently, from bow to stern with compartments opening off of it. At the foot of the stairs, slightly forward, a compartment door was open and from there I heard the sound of voices. I went down the rest of the way and tried the knob on the compartment next door. It turned easily and when I stepped into the dark room I knew it was empty. An empty room feels different. It was as I'd hoped. Like many boats, ventilation grates were installed near the ceiling, connecting one room to another, relieving the closeness of belowdecks confinement with a little air circulation. The grate was open. I pulled a chair over and stood on it and looked through.

They were all assembled, Bonsentir, Carmen Sternwood, and a tall, soft-looking guy with a lot of curly hair and big horn-rimmed glasses, who had to be Randolph Simpson. They were seated on cushions on the floor, gathered around a low table with an engraved brass top, eating with their fingers. What they were eating appeared to be some sort of grain with fruit mixed in. It looked messy to eat with your fingers, but none of them seemed to care. Carmen was wearing loose silk trousers and a silk figured top that left her middle uncovered. She didn't from where I was standing appear to have a jewel in her navel. She ate with one hand and with the other twirled wisps of Simpson's hair and then untwirled them. Clever girl, our Carmen. Never at a loss to be entertaining. She wore no shoes and her toenails had been painted blue. Occasionally she would stop twirling Simpson's hair long enough to feed a small morsel to a yellow tiger kitten who would lick her fingers eagerly each time and then be disappointed in what he found and sit back and meow. Simpson wore a flowered shirt hanging outside of white duck pants. Bonsentir wore the same white linen suit I'd seen when he left Resthaven this morning. He leaned across the table and poured some reddish liquid into Carmen's glass from a crystal flagon. She drank some and giggled. Her eyes were very wide and almost all pupil. And there was a sick bubbly sound to the giggle that went very well with the faint medicinal smell that drifted through the vent from the room. There were silk brocade hangings around the room and a bunch of flowering plants in big pots here and there. Simpson was staring at Bonsentir, and it was his voice that I heard, deep and full of overtones, like a B-movie version of God speaking from the clouds.

"You are too powerful, Randolph, he can't touch you. No one can. We can go on with our life as we have."

Simpson gazed at him like the extras in ill-fitting sandals and moth-eaten robes would have looked at God in the B-movie. He drank some of the reddish liquid from his glass. Carmen scooped some rice and fruit off the platter with the first three fingers of her right hand and shoveled it into

Simpson's mouth. He swallowed most of it, let a little of it dribble onto his shirt. Carmen wiped it away with a cerise silk napkin. And fed a crumb to the eager kitten.

"He won't stop," Simpson said. "He keeps coming around, asking questions. He found the old mine."

"He's a little man," Bonsentir intoned, "a *little* man. We will simply swat him, the way flies are swatted."

I felt a small catch in my throat. They were talking about me.

Simpson's high voice was a little shaky. He stared at Bonsentir, leaning a little toward him. Carmen ran her hand along his thigh and took a single grape from the platter and popped it in her mouth. She chewed it slowly while she rubbed her cheek against Simpson's left arm. The kitten meowed.

"He found the *mine*. He and that nosy old woman at the newspaper."

"He found nothing that matters. You have the force, Randolph. You have the power and I know it and can bring it out of you."

"And the plan," Simpson squeaked. "He's been up to Neville Valley and he's been to the Springs. He *knows*."

Bonsentir took Simpson's right hand in both of his and squeezed them.

"I'll have him removed, Randolph. He annoys you. I'll have him removed."

"What if he told?"

"Who would he tell? The police? We own the police, Randolph. We own the mayor and the governor and the legislature. This is ours, Randolph. California belongs to you."

They were silent, Bonsentir holding Simpson's hand.

"Yes!" Simpson's voice lost its squeaky plaintive trill. Carmen rubbed her cheek against his arm and her hand along his thigh. The kitten meowed again. Simpson glanced at it with irritation.

"When you sent the men," Simpson said, "you told me they'd make him stop." The voice began to slide back up to whiny again. "And he didn't. And you sent the men to Vivian and she said he didn't even work for her and even when they were hurting her she said that. And he wouldn't stop. I don't like that!"

"What did they do to Vivian?" Carmen said and giggled again, the bubbling corrupt giggle that sometimes I still hear in my dreams. Neither Simpson nor Bonsentir paid her any attention.

"He'll not disturb you further," Bonsentir said.

Carmen stopped running her hand along Simpson's thigh and put her peculiar little thumb in her mouth and began to suck it turning it a little, this way and that, as if to get all the flavor out of it.

"Is it that you are going to kill him?" she said, her head still pressed to Simpson's shoulder.

Simpson smiled at her like he was her grandpapa. "Would you like to help us?"

Carmen's bubbly giggle erupted and sustained as she nodded her head, quite solemnly, her thumb still in her mouth, her big eyes as empty as a haunted house.

"Carmen *likes* that," she said and opened her mouth and displayed her sharp little shiny teeth.

"I know," Simpson said, his voice now low and calm. "And I like Carmen."

She got up then and kissed him on top of his head.

"Carmen has to go to the little girls' room for a minute," she said and flitted gaily out of the stateroom, as carefree as a monarch butterfly. Simpson watched her go and then looked at Bonsentir. The kitten meowed and rubbed along Bonsentir's thigh. He stared at it for a moment with distaste. Then he stood suddenly and picked the kitten up by the neck. The kitten screeched. Simpson took one long-legged stride across the room and threw the kitten out the open porthole. Then he turned back and sat down.

"Soon," he said, his tone dark and very guttural. "I feel it coming on. Soon it will be Carmen's time."

"She has lasted longer than many," Bonsentir said.

"I like to think — " Simpson said, the words oozing out of him like some viscous effluent. "I like to think of her face the first moment when she knows, when she realizes what will happen to her."

Both men were silent, admiring the thought. Then the door opened and Carmen floated in again.

"All done," she announced and plumped herself back down beside Simpson, and leaned her head against his fleshy shoulder. He tilted her chin up with one hand and kissed her hard on the mouth. She wriggled her little body, excitedly, like a fish on a hook.

I got down from my chair and moved to the door and opened it a crack. It was time to take her out of there. The corridor was empty. I opened the door wider and stepped through. I took the three steps down to the next door and put my hand inside my coat for my gun. Suddenly a steel cable, thicker than the ones on which they hung the Brooklyn Bridge, went around my neck, and a vise clamped on my gun hand. I could smell the owner, it was the Mexican. And it wasn't a steel cable, it was his forearm. I tried to stamp on his instep but the cable around my neck kept tightening. I jammed my left elbow back into his ribs. It had as much effect as if I'd slugged him with a marsh-mallow. I could feel the pressure build in my head. I couldn't see anything but a reddish haze. My gun and gun hand were still im-mobile under my coat. I tried to bend forward and throw him but it was like trying to bend an oak tree. I couldn't breathe. The reddish haze got darker and redder and finally enveloped me and I plunged into it and dis-appeared.

32

I woke up sitting on the floor in a bright little room with no furniture. I closed my eyes for a moment and opened them again. There was a strong light shining in my face. My neck hurt, my head throbbed, I was aware that the reassuring weight of my gun was gone from under my left arm. I squinted past the light and could make out forms, not very clearly. One of them was surely the Mexican with his huge upper body and long arms. Others I couldn't make out. My mouth felt as if I'd eaten a blotter.

"He appears to have regained consciousness." It was the voice of Dr. Bonsentir, descending from the clouds. "How convenient of you, Mr. Marlowe, to have come to us, just when we had decided we must find you."

I braced my feet and edged my back up the wall and got myself standing. The Mexican moved out from behind the light and stepped closer to me. I could see my gun stuck in his belt. At least he hadn't tied a knot in the barrel.

"Why don't we just kill him right now." Simpson's voice came deep and thick from the darkness. "Then we won't have to think about it anymore."

I heard Carmen's suppurating giggle.

"I think it would be better," Bonsentir said, "to wait until we put out to sea again. It will make disposal of the body safer and less troublesome."

"I don't like to sail at night," Simpson said. His voice was back up again. It had the petulant ring of a kid who didn't want to go to bed early.

"I know, Randolph. It's all right. We'll keep him here until we get under way in the morning."

"It's too late," I said. "Too many people know."

"Who knows?" Simpson said. "I told you, Claude, he told people. Who knows? What do they know?" His voice went up and down like a piccolo solo.

"He would say that, Randolph. He's in profound jeopardy and he knows it. He would say that and hope it would save him, but it won't."

"The DA's chief investigator, Bernie Ohls, knows it," I said. "And the DA, Taggert Wilde, and the San Bernardino DA's office, and a Missing Persons' cop named Gregory, and a hard case named Eddie Mars who right now is maybe a hundred yards away with a boatload of tough boys who are ready to come over here and shoot your ears off."

"I know Eddie Mars," Carmen said excitedly. Oh boy! A familiar name.

Simpson came around into the lamplight. His soft face was red.

"Stop it," he said, his voice fluting down the scale as he spoke. It was eerie to hear, and at another time it would have been an interesting phenomenon. "You're trying to frighten me. Nobody knows. They can't. I'm too powerful. No one can know about me. So just shut your mouth, because you're going to be killed." The last sentence bottomed off into darkness.

My head felt like it was ready to rupture and my neck hurt and my throat was sore and I was a little dizzy, and sick of the light in my eyes and sick of being yammered at by an oversized brat. I hit him. It was a pretty good punch given the shape I was in. I felt his nose flatten and saw blood come. He screamed with a sound like glass shattering and stumbled back with his hands to his face and the blood running between his fingers, and kept screaming in high sharp bursts, like a European fire engine: *whoop, whoop, whoop*! I turned toward the Mex and

something hit the side of my head and I
went back once again to a place I'd been
spending too much time in.

33

This time when I came around I was alone. The only light came from a small bulb in the ceiling. All the parts that had hurt before hurt worse, and in addition I had an aching bruise on the left side of my jaw just in front of my ear. I sat for a while, fighting nausea. There was no movement in the yacht other than the slight toss of the easy swells on which we rode. Through the porthole I could see that it was still dark. Time to stand up. I could do it. Six feet tall, 190 pounds. In top condition. I could just stand right up. I tried to get my legs under me and they felt like seaweed. I compromised by inching over against the wall and slowly sitting up with my back supported by the wall. Even the dim light hurt my eyes. I squinted. Maybe I wouldn't get up just yet. Instead I'd survey the room, while I rested. There wasn't much to survey. Whatever light had shone in my eyes was gone, as was all the furniture. There was another flowering tropical plant growing in a big pot in the corner, and two throw pillows that might have been on a couch at one time. Other than that I was in an empty steel room painted ivory, with a porthole too small to squeeze through.

My watch was broken, probably smashed when I fell, I didn't know which time. I'd been falling so much that it could have happened anytime. There was a smear of blood on my shirt that must have gushed from Simpson's nose when I'd hit him. I took some satisfaction in that. Painfully, with rest stops often, I got to my feet. The room spun. I hung there for a moment, teetering over the void. Then it stabilized. I was up. I edged along the wall to the door and tried it. It was locked. Surprise! There was no other way out. I looked at the potted plant. It was real, growing in dirt. With a big purple trumpet-shaped flower on it. If you were as rich as Randolph Simpson you could have flowering plants grow anywhere you wanted.

I looked at the plant for a minute and then sat down on the floor again, and held steady until the room stopped spinning, and took off my right shoe and sock. I put the shoe back on my sockless foot and slowly got to my feet again. I was getting the hang of it. Someday I'd probably be able to do it whenever I wanted to. If there was going to be a someday. Carefully I filled the sock about two-thirds full of dirt from the pot. Then I tied a knot in it and slapped it gently across my hand. It felt about right. I walked to the porthole and opened it and took a couple of deep breaths of cool sea air. Then I went back and stood against the wall next to the door where it latched and with my left hand began to bang on the door.

"Let me out," I hollered as loud as I could. "Let me out of here!"

I had to holler it several more times and keep banging on the door before I heard footsteps in the corridor and a jangle of keys and the door swung open. The Mexican came in with my gun still stuck in his belt and I laid the dirt-filled sock carefully against the side of his head back of his left ear. Very hard. He grunted and stumbled forward and went to his knees and I hit him again with my homemade sap, square across the back of the head this time, and he sighed and pitched face forward onto the floor. I kicked him hard in the head and then crouched beside him and got my hand under him and pulled my gun loose from his belt. The keys he'd used to open my door were sprawled five feet in front of his outflung hand. I picked them up and went into the corridor and locked the door behind me. I had the reassuring weight of the gun again, and this time I kept it in my hand. So many people had taken it away from me, I barely recognized it.

The corridor was empty and silent. The doors that lined it were closed. I went along the corridor, listening at each door. There were no sounds except snoring in one cabin. There was no way to know who was snoring. I continued along, and at the last door on the port side I heard the familiar giggle. I tried the door. It was locked. I looked at the lock and tried a key that looked like it would match from the key ring I'd taken from the Mex. It fit and I opened the door gently.

Carmen was there all right, and Simpson. The lights were on. He was handcuffed to the bed, facedown, and Carmen, in a condition I was beginning to tire of, was naked as a minnow. She stood over Simpson, giggling her giggle and spanking him with a gold-inlaid ivory hairbrush.

I closed the door softly behind me and stepped into the room. Carmen looked up with her big eyes all iris and smiled.

"I know you," she said. "You've got the funny name."

"Doghouse Reilly," I said.

Simpson turned his head to look at me

and I smiled at the thick white tape over his nose and the beginnings of a wonderful pair of shiners starting to darken under his eyes. He opened his mouth and I stepped over and put the gun barrel into it.

"Not a peep," I said.

His eyes widened but he was silent. Without clothing, his soft body was fleshy and white. I looked around the room. On the wall next to the bed, hanging on a hook, was a lacy peignoir. With the gun still in Simpson's mouth, I said to Carmen, "Put that robe on."

She smiled at me that loopy void smile that she had and put her thumb in her mouth. As always, it was supposed to make me jump in the air and click my heels. As always, it didn't work.

"If you make a sound I'll kill you," I said.

I took the gun out of Simpson's mouth and went and got the peignoir off the hook and slipped my gun under my arm while I forced Carmen's arms through the sleeves and buttoned the two buttons, which didn't do a very good job of holding the thing together. There was a sash, too, and I tied it around her waist. Then I took my gun out from under my arm again, pulled the sheet and two blankets up over Simpson's head, took a firm grip on Carmen's wrist, and went out of the room and into the corridor. As I closed the door behind me I heard Simpson, muffled through two blankets, yell "Help!" Five feet down the corridor I couldn't hear him.

"Where are we going?" Carmen said. She didn't seem scared. She seemed excited. Her lips were pulled back over her small white teeth. They were sharp teeth and whiter than teeth had any business being.

"Home," I said.

We went up the ladder well to the deck, with my gun in my right hand and my left with a death grip on Carmen's wrist. On deck there was only the boy in the sailor suit at the stern, gazing out over the black water at the shoreline.

"Shhh," I said to Carmen.

She giggled, her little sharp teeth showing even in the pale moonlight, and screamed as loud as she could. The boy in the sailor suit whirled, clawing at the gun in its regulation holster. I fired once and he yelped and staggered against the rail and then pitched forward. I heard doors open below me and footsteps on the ladder wells. I dragged Carmen to the rail and stowed my gun again under my arm. Behind me I heard the hatchway open and someone yelling,

"Over there, by the rail."

I got my arms around Carmen's waist and heaved her up. She screamed again and I pitched her over the rail into the darkness, and dove after her. The water stung when I hit the surface and then I was in it and went under maybe ten or fifteen feet before I was able to turn and start up. My wet clothes dragged me back, and the weight of the gun under my arm was no longer comforting. My lungs had already been abused once this evening and they didn't enjoy further abuse. At about the time I began to get the panicky feeling that I wouldn't make it to the surface, I did, and came back into the world in the ebony water and started looking for Carmen. I saw her twenty feet away, floundering. I swam toward her as someone on the yacht began to sweep the water with a flashlight. It must have been one of those long affairs with six batteries, because the beam was strong and the circle of light was large. I reached Carmen, who was giggling and crying and spluttering at the same time. The flashlight swept by us and started back and then Blondie was there in the skiff and reaching for Carmen. The light hit us and a shot splashed the water near the skiff and then from somewhere in the darkness south of us a chatter of shots sounded and bullets spanged off the hull of the yacht and the flashlight went out and someone yelled, "Get down!" Then Carmen was in, and I was, rolling in over the gunwales of the skiff without quite knowing how I had and Blondie was silently pulling in the direction of the gunfire.

"I never thought I'd be glad to see you," I said to him.

"Sure," he said.

34

"I don't want to go home," Carmen said. She was sitting with a blanket wrapped around her in the tiny belowdecks stateroom of Mars' cabin cruiser. We were heading for the landing pier in the very earliest gray hint of dawn. Simpson's yacht had too much draft to follow us in. It was under full power, running north around the point.

I was there with my jacket off but the rest of me still soaking wet and Mars was looking fresh and comfortable as he leaned against the bulkhead.

"I still say we should have gone in and finished it," Mars said.

"Bad idea, Eddie. Simpson's got about a regiment with him whenever he travels. You'd have gotten wiped out."

"I got some pretty good boys with me, soldier."

"We came for Carmen," I said. "We've got her."

"I don't *want* to go home," Carmen said.

"It's not going to end here, soldier."

"I know," I said. "We have assault

charges, and kidnapping, illegal restraint, attempted murder, murder, probably two counts. We have a witness." I nodded toward Carmen.

"Not much of a witness," Mars said. "You think you can make any of them stick against Simpson?"

"If we ever get Simpson alone," I said, "in a quiet room, with maybe a couple of tough cops who know how it's done, he'll babble like a brook. It's Bonsentir that keeps him together."

"You know any tough cops like that?" Mars said.

"One or two," I said. "When we get ashore I'll call one."

"Be a good thing," Mars said, "if you kinda leave me out of it. Cops would like to tag me anyway, and what we pulled off here may not be exactly one hundred percent legal."

"I'll do what I can," I said. "I owe you that much."

"You don't owe me a thing, soldier. I wasn't doing it for you."

"I'll keep you out of it anyway."

The cabin cruiser slowed to an idle and bumped gently broadside against the landing. It was early dawn and the sky was a lighter gray in the east. I collected Carmen and went ashore to find my car and find a phone and make a phone call.

Which I did.

35

We were in a brightly lighted clean gray room in the Coast Guard Station in Long Beach. Ohls was there smoking one of his toy cigars and looking as if he'd had a good breakfast. There was also a captain from the Long Beach police, who was tall and thin and had a big Adam's apple and the expression of a man who didn't like his job. Behind a neat gray government-issue desk was a Coast Guard lieutenant commander named Fenton, who had a red face and the upper body of a beer barrel. I sat on a straight chair in front of the commander. Carmen, dressed in a Coast Guard fatigue shirt and dungarees four sizes too big, looked like Mary Pickford on the chair beside me. Ohls was standing near the doorway, and the Long Beach police captain, whose name was Rackley, was leaning on the wall next to Fenton's desk.

"We don't need her," Ohls said. "We brought Simpson into the Coast Guard brig and he wouldn't shut up. He told us about the Neville Valley water scheme. He told us about chopping up Lola Monforte and four or five others from all over the country. He told us that Dr. Bonsentir was with him in everything and was his, ah, 'mentor' I think he called him, and 'spiritual adviser.' "

"Where's Bonsentir?" I said.

Ohls looked at Fenton.

"Had a Mexican with him," Fenton said. "Built like a gorilla. He put up a fight — trying to protect Bonsentir, I guess. I got a seaman in the hospital and another with a broken arm. The chief in charge of the detail had to shoot him dead."

"And?"

"And in the scuffle Bonsentir disappeared."

"He'll turn up," Ohls said. "We cut off his juice anyway, with Simpson."

"Can I see Randolph?" Carmen said.

"Not right now," Ohls said. He looked at me. "We got your statement, Marlowe, and hers. And before Simpson stops talking we may get him for murdering Lincoln."

I nodded. Carmen was working on her thumb again.

"Wait a minute," Rackley said. His Adam's apple juggled up and down his thin neck. "Are you turning them loose?"

"Yeah."

"Long Beach might have something to say about that," Rackley said.

"Long Beach would still be tripping over its own handcuffs, if Fenton here hadn't made a courtesy call," Ohls said. "Nothing going on here happened in Long Beach."

"I resent the crack about the handcuffs," Rackley said.

"I was kinda hoping you would," Ohls said. "You got any problems letting them walk?" He looked at Fenton.

"We're going to need her, it comes to trial," Fenton said. "Him too."

"Look," Ohls said patiently. "This guy goes out by himself onto a boat full of guys with big guns to rescue a nymphomaniac lulu that's sicker than two buzzards. He gets strangled and sapped and damn nears drowns and gets her out and brings her to us. He also solves a noisy dismemberment murder for us and prevents somebody from stealing a lifetime supply of water from some people up north."

Ohls took a puff on his toy cigar and took it out of his mouth and looked at it for a moment.

"For this he gets paid . . . how much you getting for this, Marlowe?"

"A dollar, and expenses."

"Tank of gas, maybe?"

"And two bullets," I said.

Ohls crossed his arms and stared at Rackley.

"You think when it comes time to testify we ain't going to find him?"

"The lieutenant has a point there," I said to Rackley.

"You think nobody helped him get on and off that yacht?" Rackley said. "Coast Guard found twenty-eight bullet holes in the hull and superstructure."

"I reload fast," I said.

"Nobody in Long Beach probably knows this," Ohls said. "But most good cops know when to press and when to leave alone. I like this thing just the way Marlowe told it."

Rackley got up.

"Hell," he said. "Like you said there's no Long Beach jurisdiction here."

He walked past me and Ohls and went out of the room and closed the door hard, but not too hard, behind him.

"You got any problems, Commander?" Ohls said.

"Let them walk," Fenton said.

"The way I figure there won't be a trial anyway," I said. "Simpson's mushier than an old apple, and his lawyers will plead him insane and it will stick."

We were on our feet now. I shook hands with Fenton.

"Where we going?" Carmen said. "I'm very sleepy."

"Home," I said. "Your maid will put you to bed."

"Not you?" she said and her tongue showed between her lips and she gave me the slow vamp, looking at me with her head turned, from the corners of her eyes.

"I'm sleepy too," I said. "I'll let the maid do it."

My car was in the parking lot, next to the black one that belonged to the county, that Ohls drove.

"Thanks, Bernie," I said.

Ohls nodded and opened his car door and paused with one foot in, leaning on the top.

"She's got to go away someplace too," he said.

"I know."

"One of us will see to it," he said. "I'd just as soon it be you. But one of us will have to."

"I'll do it," I said.

I opened my door and Carmen got in. I closed it after her and went around to the driver's side. Ohls was still halfway in his car, still leaning on the roof.

"Bonsentir's going to come for you," Ohls said.

"Yeah," I said.

"Sooner or later," Ohls said.

"Good," I said. "He'll think he went head-first into a Mixmaster."

Ohls nodded slowly and got in his car and started up and drove away. I watched him go. Then I got in beside Carmen, and cranked the engine, and started out toward Hollywood, with my eyes heavier than sorrow. And the rest of me no better.

36

"So you did it," Vivian Regan said.

I was sitting in her enormous living room in the middle of the morning with my feet up on a hassock. I put my head back against the big leather wing chair I was sitting in and let my eyes close. My clothes had dried on me and I looked like something that had washed up in a storm drain. I felt worse.

"I was sure they'd kill you," Vivian said.

"Wrong," I said.

"Yes, I was. And I'm awfully glad I was."

"Yeah."

The stillness in the house seemed essential, part of the substance of the house, integrated with the floor joists and ceiling rafters, impregnating the plaster. Vivian sat with her legs tucked up under her on the vast overstuffed lavender silk couch across from me. She had on some sort of black silk lounging pajamas and a string of pearls, the kind you keep in the vault, and wear paste.

"Will you help me with Carmen?" she said.

"I'll find her a place and see that she is admitted and that she stays," I said.

"Will she have to go to trial?"

"I don't think so. I doubt there'll be a trial. I think this will all be discreetly arranged and she and Simpson will both be judged insane and put into custodial care."

Vivian shivered and hugged herself.

"Insane," she said. "It's such an awful word."

I didn't say anything. Vivian stood and walked over and stood behind me and massaged my neck and shoulders.

"What about us, Marlowe? We had something the other night."

I nodded.

"There'd be room here for you, you know."

"For a while," I said.

"You don't think it would last?"

"You're scared now. You're alone. You've got Carmen to worry over again. You don't know where Bonsentir is. Someone like me looks pretty good now. But how would I look next year? How would I look at the polo matches? Do I get my own monogrammed blazer? Do I take elocution lessons so I can sound like a phony Englishman and fit in with the clubhouse crowd at Del Mar?"

"You simply are a bastard, aren't you, Marlowe."

"I'm a detective, lady. I told you that before. I don't play at it. I work at it. I belong where I am, in a lousy apartment

272

on Franklin, in a crummy office on Cahuenga. I pay my own way, and do what I will do, and don't accept insults. It isn't much. But it's mine. Whatever brains and guts and muscle I was dealt, it belongs to me, and I use it in my work. And what money I have I earned."

She was crying. I felt a little like crying myself.

She said, "Do you want to kiss me goodbye?"

I said, "I want to kiss you goodbye," and dragged myself to my feet and put my arms around her and she pressed against me and opened her mouth and we kissed for a long time. Then we broke and she said, "Don't come back. I couldn't stand it again," and turned and left the room fast. I stood and tried to get my breathing calm.

While I was doing that, Norris came into the room.

"Mrs. Regan asked me to show you out, sir."

"On my way," I said.

"I'm very grateful, sir, that Miss Carmen is back."

"We'll see to a proper place for her, Norris."

"Yes, sir, the General would approve of that, sir."

I said, "Norris, do you have champagne?"

"Yes, sir."

"Chilled?" I said.

"Of course, sir."

"Bring it with some brandy," I said, "and two glasses, to the greenhouse, please."

Norris smiled. "Yes, sir," he said.

The greenhouse was as I remembered it. Stifling, thick with moisture, overgrown with thick fleshy plants. In the center, just as it had been, was the wheelchair on the red Turkish rug on the flagstones under the domed roof. The lap robe was folded and hung over the back. There were two wicker chairs set near the wheelchair. Drops of water fell from the glass roof and splattered occasionally on the hexagonal flagstones. I sat in one of the wicker chairs and took out a cigarette and lit it and exhaled slowly. Norris came through the jungle pushing a tea wagon with a bottle of French champagne in a silver ice bucket, which was already densely beaded, and a bottle of fine French brandy.

"The champagne as cold as Valley Forge," I said to Norris, "and about a third of a glass of brandy beneath it."

Norris didn't speak, but he mixed two glasses of champagne and brandy and handed me one. We drank in silence. The forest dripped, the smell of the orchids was like the smell of dying beauty, *the rotten sweetness of a prostitute,* General Sternwood had said.

We finished our drink without a word. Norris standing, me sitting in the wicker chair where I had sat the first time I'd met the General.

"He had the soldier's eye, Norris," I said. "Like yours."

"If I may say so, sir," Norris said, "not unlike yours."

Then we put our glasses down on the tea wagon and I shook Norris's hand and walked away from there. On the way out I saw Eddie Mars get out of his car and stroll to the front door. He didn't see me. I walked out to the street past the slow sweep of the lawn sprinkler and got in my car and drove away and didn't look back.

THORNDIKE PRESS hopes you have enjoyed this Large Print book. All our Large Print titles are designed for easy reading, and all our books are made to last. Other Thorndike Large Print books are available at your library, through selected bookstores, or directly from the publisher. For more information about current and upcoming titles, please call or mail your name and address to:

THORNDIKE PRESS
PO Box 159
Thorndike, Maine 04986
800/223-6121
207/948-2962